PUNISHMENT

Linda Rocker

Punishment

Published by Wheatmark®
1760 E. River Road, Suite 145,
Tucson, Arizona 85718 U.S.A.
www.wheatmark.com

ISBN: 978-1-60494-763-2
LCCN: 2012939834

For
Harriet & Manny

*"If you are acquainted with the principle,
what do you care for a
myriad instances and applications?"*

—Henry David Thoreau
Where I Lived, and What I Lived For

AUTHOR'S NOTE

THIS IS A work of fiction. Although it is impossible for a writer to completely distance herself from her life experiences, I have taken great pains to avoid the use of specific incidents, parties and cases in my writing, especially those that are not part of a public record. Any case or character that appears in the story and has also appeared in my life is an amalgamation of that which is known and that which may be discovered by research about similar cases and characters.

Punishment is the first of a trilogy of novels meant to explore and challenge what we believe our system of justice should be about, how it should function, where it succeeds, and how it fails. On a deeper level, I hope my readers will be drawn to the question of who is punished, why and how they are punished, and whether we are satisfied. These lofty ambitions were nurtured by people close to me, many of whom were delighted to see such philosophical questions emerge in the form of legal thriller, not a treatise.

I'm indebted to my dearest collaborator and personal editor, my husband Dan Silverberg, and my children, Sara, Mike, Matt, Julie, Adam, and Belinda, who did me the greatest favor by taking me seriously. Many friends took time to read and comment on part or all of the manuscript and I thank them all—that means you, Elaine Shindler, Casey Portman, Sandy Underhill, Peter Hearn, Iudita Harlan, Ina Yalof, Lee Ballard, Norman Wain, and Cynthia Dettelbach.

Janice Eidus is my mentor, my editor, and my best critic. As an acclaimed author of numerous novels and short stories, she has inspired and amazed me with her insights into the role of the reader, truly an art form in and of itself.

My publisher, Wheatmark, my webmaster, Monkey-CMedia, and my marketing guru, Penny Sansevieri, have brought incredible enthusiasm to our work and have shown equally incredible patience with my technological ineptness.

Finally, I want to thank Chief Judge Peter Blanc of the Circuit Court in West Palm Beach for spending time with me to answer my questions about the court and its procedures. I have tried to faithfully incorporate Florida law and to accurately describe the courthouse setting. Some adjustments to location and personnel were required for security reasons and, in the case of job descriptions and titles, for simplicity. So to all of you who see my goofs, my gaffes, and my gall, kindly follow my dear, departed mother's admonition, "If you don't have something nice to say, say nothing at all."

P.S. Be sure to read the prologue and the first three chapters of *Blame*, the second in this trilogy, which you'll find at the back of the book. Enjoy!

| 1 |

THE SENSATION OF being airborne came before the sound of shattering glass. Casey felt the floor shake with the force of the blast. Over the succeeding years, with each recitation of that day's events, she would marvel at the complete lack of any premonition, the absolute absence of any clue of the mayhem that was about to unfold in the sunshine capital of the world.

She had arrived at the parking garage of the Justice Complex with at least five minutes to spare. If she could somehow manage to get through to the elevators without breathing the dust and grime, she would have just enough time to get a large coffee at the Blind Stand. It was a cool day, unusually so for Florida at this time of year, and she was

1

dressed in what was equally unusual casual attire. Her work as bailiff to Judge Janet Kanterman did not require a Brooks Brothers look, but she was expected to look businesslike. The pink, low-cut camisole under the cropped sweater and white jeans was definitely not businesslike. She hoped the trial scheduled for today would not go forward. The last thing she needed was a bunch of lawyers teasing her about "dress down" days. Maybe the defendant would cop a plea, but that was unlikely. The prosecutors were playing deal or no deal, and this jerk's only offer from the State was to roll for murder two—a guaranteed fifteen years without parole.

She passed the guard stationed near the garage entrance to the courthouse. This particular guy never looked her in the eye, but he always looked her over.

"Morning, Ed," she said, purposely angling her body away from his view as she went through the altar-like metal detector. With his eyes focused on her backside, Ed nodded. After she was almost beyond the reach of his words, he called, "Looking good, Casey. Looking real good."

She made her way to the bank of elevators that carried judges, bailiffs, and other court personnel to the dozens of courtrooms in the twelve-story building. The first three floors were dedicated to public business such as the traffic bureau, the clerk of courts, the title offices, and so forth. These were the floors where you could hear yourself think. Even the public areas were quiet compared to the floors where people came to get copies of outstanding warrants or pay fines so they could spring a loved one from the jail located several miles away on a street with the unlikely name of Gun Club Road.

People milled around Jake's, a small, cafeteria-style eatery that was definitely not a place for people on a diet. They formed small circles around the efficient and very well-dressed criminal lawyers and spoke in loud voices on their cell phones, mixing the accents of transplanted New

Yorkers with farmers; the drawl of purebred Southerners with the smooth, moist music of the South Americans and the patois of a sizeable black Caribbean population that now dominated the small enclaves of affordable homes in the downtown area.

Casey enjoyed a number of special privileges accorded to bailiffs, including liberal access to the building and occasional lunches in the judges' dining room. What's more, the pay was decent for a job with every weekend and holiday off, but when court was in session, the work was intense. In addition to knowing the individual needs and wishes of each judge, including what they liked for lunch and who they took calls from on their private lines, a bailiff was expected to clear with the judge and post outside the courtroom door the schedule for all hearings and trials, to contact attorneys for special meetings or motions, and to be the conduit for all the interactions with the clerk's office and the deputy sheriffs. Of greatest importance, however, was the bailiff's responsibility to maintain order in the courtroom. It was not a job for the faint of heart or for people with oversized egos. Casey was good at her job, and she loved it. She also loved her morning coffee. Casey looked at her watch and made a quick decision to wait until later for the coffee. Judge Kanterman was forgiving of many mistakes and shortcomings, but being late was not one of them.

"Hey, Ms. Casey Portman! How goes it, girl?" A tall, pencil-thin black man appeared beside her. Casey was always happy to see her fellow bailiff, Benjamin Toledo, a law student who worked for one of for the other judges on the fourth floor.

"It goes well, Ben. It goes exceedingly well," Casey replied, stepping into the elevator and briskly swiping her card against the reader. As the elevator doors silently slid and joined, she couldn't help noticing the Krispy Kreme bag tucked against Ben's chest between the manila files. Her sigh was audible. Ben caught it and grinned at her. They had been friends for a while now, and he knew that Casey took pains to stay in shape; her daily dose of pain, as she put it to him, included watching Ben eat all the fattening foods she craved but denied herself. Obviously today would be no exception. At nearly six feet, she had broad shoulders that made her feel like a linebacker in everything she wore. Surprisingly, the rest of her body was lean and well proportioned. Almost twenty-eight, she retained a full complement of freckles, framed by strong brows and curly brown hair. An attractive package overall, but no cover girl kind of looks.

"Hey, Case, are you guys going to trial in that murder case today? I got a call from Channel 5 asking if they could stash some equipment in Judge Clarke's chambers during the trial." Ben's judge, Barbara Clarke, was on special assignment to the First District Court of Appeals in Tallahassee. She'd been gone for nearly a month, and the other trial judges had tried to divide up her docket of cases as evenly as possible. Because Casey's judge was on the same floor, they seemed to get more than their share.

"If it goes to trial, we'll need to limit the media to a pool rep. Probably Court TV. The security problems on this one will be over the top." Casey stepped out of the elevator and turned to face Ben. It was exactly 9:01 am when the blast rocked the building.

"Casey, look at me. Are you okay? Open your eyes, for chrissakes!" Ben's face was literally on hers, and she found herself unable to get a deep breath. She instinctively pushed her hands on his chest and turned her face away. Ben rolled off her and got to his knees beside her. "You've got some blood on your forehead. Any idea where it's coming from?"

"Yeah, idiot." Casey looked in his face. "From your bloody nose." As Ben reached up toward his nose, Casey pulled herself away from him and up onto her elbows. She began to take in the turmoil around her. Children were shrieking wildly, inconsolably, while most of the adults were either seated on the floor with dazed expressions or shouting into cell phones. Incredibly, other than Ben's bloody nose, there did not appear to be a lot of injuries. That was in part because the thick glass windows that lined the hallways outside the courtrooms as protection from a hurricane had held firm, unlike the smaller windows that lay in shards around the area.

The sirens from below as police cars rushed back to the building were only background sound for the piercing noise of the fire alarms sounding all over the building.

"Casey. Come here. I need you right now."

Casey turned, recognizing the judge's voice. Janet Kanterman should have come out of her mother's womb wearing a judge's robe. She was perfect for her role in life in every respect, although the people who had known her as a child reported that she had seemed too quiet and too withdrawn for any career but a librarian. Janet, herself, loved to recount her transformation after she had discovered the debate team in high school. She quickly gained a reputation for a steel-trap memory and a passion to win her point that earned her the nickname "Barracuda."

But at this moment, Judge Kanterman was anything but deadly. She had rushed from her courtroom into the hallway and was on the floor, holding two small, screaming children on her lap and rocking them back and forth. She looked up at her bailiff.

"Casey, we need to get some control of this situation. Please have everyone who doesn't require medical help evacuated immediately. I know we may destroy some evidence, but I need, repeat, I need and must have everyone out of this building. Got it?"

"Done," said Casey, matching her boss's urgent tone. She headed toward the group of police officers near the elevators. "The judge has ordered the building cleared without delay. No elevators, only the stairs. She wants everyone out of here in the next five minutes. Got it?" she asked, praying that her tough manner would mask her shaking hands and tear-filled eyes. "This happens in the movies," she muttered to herself, "or in New York or LA. Not in goddamn small-town America!"

As people stood and moved away from the walls that they still clung to for protection, Casey surveyed the surroundings more closely. Her passion for solving mysteries as a child—everything from finding a lost cat to locating the missing remote—meant that her parents were not at all surprised that she now worked in the criminal justice system. True to form, Casey was looking hard at the people milling about the floor, some of whom were still dazed and disbelieving. She flirted with the idea of asking the staff from the other courtrooms if they had seen anything or anyone who seemed especially suspicious. She would need to emphasize "especially," since courthouses are natural settings for the daily appearance of some unusual and strangely attired people. But this was not a time for questions. The judge was right. The evacuation was necessary in case another blast was imminent, even if it meant destroying evidence—evidence that might point to the perpetrators.

Casey moved toward the stragglers and urged them toward the staircase. No one set off her personal radar for suspects, but then she was still blurry-minded herself and figured that whoever had caused this was probably long gone.

By noon, the building was nearly deserted except for news crews hanging around hoping for something to spice up drive time. The judges had gathered in a conference room on the first floor of the nearby police station. For most of the judges, it was their first visit to the building on Banyon Road, and it was easy to read the discomfort on their faces and in their body language. Judge Spellman, the presiding judge at the court, had been in private practice before being appointed and then elected to the bench. If any of his clients had ever seen the inside of a lockup, it would be a surprise to him. Even though Judge Marks and Judge Helberg had practiced criminal defense law, the smells and scenes were as unfamiliar to them as they were to the rest of the court personnel in attendance.

"Let's begin this meeting so we can get out of this place as soon as possible," said Judge Spellman, surveying the scratched, coffee-stained blonde wood conference table around which sat more than a half-dozen of the Criminal Court judges. "Judge Clarke's bailiff informs me that she is on her way back from Tallahassee and will arrive this evening." Spellman nodded toward Ben, who was seated at the back of the room along with the other bailiffs.

"We're all shocked at what has happened, but we're also grateful that nobody was seriously hurt," Spellman continued. "I've asked Chief Anderson to address us and tell us what, if anything, the police know so far."

Casey looked up as Luke Anderson walked to the front of the room. Anderson was known throughout Central Florida as "a cops' cop." He couldn't be bought by anyone, even through his was an elected job and unemployment was as near as the next voting day. His dark-brown crew cut never varied, nor did his athletic build, but time had added a pronounced network of lines around his face and neck.

"I wish I had some hard information for you folks, but we know very little at this point. We do know how it was done. If you remember the first bombing at the twin towers in New York, then you know that the bomb in that case was planted in a van in the underground garage of the building. The saving grace there was the structure of the basement at the point of impact. A lot of power was absorbed and deflected. That is pretty much what happened here, except that this exploding device wasn't much more than an over-sized cherry bomb, so it didn't do much damage at all."

"You mean physical damage, right, Chief? 'Cause as far as I'm concerned, this incident has scared the crap out of everybody—me included." Judge Marks was clearly agitated, and he swung around in his seat to face Judge Spellman. "Who's kidding whom here? This wasn't a jailbreak out of the Wild West. The damn police are over here—not there! This is a threat to one of us, and it doesn't take a genius to figure out who that is."

Chief Anderson cleared his throat. "Unfortunately, Your Honor, any conclusions as to motive or perpetrators at this point would be premature and pure speculation."

Despite the Chief's cautionary words, everyone in the room had turned toward Judge Kanterman. After all, it wasn't every day that the state brought murder charges against a guy on the theory that he had used his pit bull dog to kill his common-law wife. The "Dogicide" case, as it had been dubbed by the media, was originally prosecuted in Miami, but the pretrial publicity was so circus-like that a change of venue was sought and granted. The fact that the victim's father was a kingpin in the auto industry and that the nature of the crime had meant excessive media coverage made it unlikely, if not impossible, to find a jury anywhere in the state with no knowledge of the case. Changes of venue were always a problem because invariably the case was moved to a smaller city with a smaller pool of potential jurors to choose from. What's more, the pretrial publicity that in years past had been confined to newspapers and mainstream televi-sion was now everywhere, unrestricted, unregulated, and unburdened by any legal limitations.

In fact, the courts in many jurisdictions have reluc-tantly concluded that cable television, in particular, has all but destroyed the ideal of an impartial jury for high-profile or sensational crimes. Nonstop coverage of trials—

complete with talking heads, live viewing, and camera-ready experts—has become the substitute for many viewers' daily dose of soap operas. Although a few bar associations have debated whether the first amendment rights of a Nancy Grace or Geraldo Rivera should be accorded greater protection than the due process rights of a defendant, especially when the stakes may be life or death, most lawyers, including the criminal defense bar, consider the ill-informed and meaningless posturing on cable TV to be harmless. "Think of the audience these shows attract," observed an adviser to the bar association. Legal experts also point to the verdicts in several high-profile trials like the Casey Anthony case as evidence that no amount of celebrity grandstanding is likely to sway a group of jurors once they have accepted such an awesome responsibility.

This particular case had landed on Kanterman's docket by a random draw, a lottery of sorts, and the other judges were either relieved that they wouldn't have to wrestle with the tough issues that would undoubtedly be raised in such a high-profile indictment, or they were drooling with envy at Kanterman's chance to make national news.

Judge Spellman rapped his knuckles on the table. "Listen, people, this is not a reality show here, and whoever went to the trouble to set off an incendiary device in a courthouse is a serious person looking to send a serious message. We're going to take it seriously as well. I suggest we leave the investigation to the Chief and turn to the more pressing need for our security in the near future."

As the discussion of body scanners and eye sensors droned on, Casey looked around the room, certain that no one else knew about the threatening letters Judge Kanterman had recently received from animal rights groups expressing fury that a dog was implicated as an accomplice or as a weapon in such a gruesome murder. If some of these correspondents had any inkling that the dog might be euthanized once they had a jury verdict, the threats were likely to inch closer to real acts of retaliation.

Casey had read a good deal of the Dogicide case file and thought that if anyone should be furious, it was Amy Cohen's parents, not a bunch of dog lovers. She wondered if the parents of a murder victim like Amy ever dreamed of revenge—the more primitive sort of revenge that made it to the movie screen, but not to a real courtroom. *I might,* Casey had thought when she put down the file, *But dreaming and doing are two very different things.*

2

IF YOU'RE THINKING about committing an interesting crime, West Palm Beach is a natural choice for location. The weather is good from October through June, and if you ignore the occasional destructive hurricane or tornado, there is little that stands between a competent killer and his prey. No nasty gloves or boots, no snow tires or scrapers, no slippery streets or sidewalks. All this environmental ease may account for a high crime rate, but the annual tide of sun seekers with deep pockets is at least as much to blame for the sobering statistics about the chances of harm on the Treasure Coast. Still, West Palm is a small town with its resident population of petty criminals, larcenous storekeepers; pill-popping, juiced-up armed robbers and crazed rapists. And then there are the regulars.

Jack McGinty was definitely one of the regulars. He had his first drink at the age of seven. His mother sent him late in the morning of that day to find his grandfather.

"Start at the Dew Drop Inn, and go in every bar on that block. You'll find him at one of them, and if you don't, then you'll have to go to the park. He'll be asleep on a bench, no doubt. And don't you show him no disrespect, neither. He's your pa's pa."

Jack retied the loose laces on his high-tops and took off at a sprint for the corner. He knew why Ma wanted Gramps back soon. Today was his sister's communion, and nothing was going to spoil Marie's big day with God—especially not an old drunk smelling of cheap scotch.

He got lucky. Gramps was on the first stool at the bar. *That was a good sign*, thought Jack. *When Gramps was really far gone, he moved to a booth, knowing that the stool was an accident waiting to happen.*

Whitey McGinty looked up just as Jack came through the door. "There's my son's son, by God, and he's come to join his old grandpappy to celebrate on this fine occasion."

Another good sign, thought Jack, *He still remembers what's happening today.*

"A wee one for Jack here," called Whitey.

The bartender looked carefully around the room. Although it was only ten in the morning, the place already reeked of stale beer and cigarettes, that olfactory trademark that distinguishes a true barroom from one of the trendy bistros that had recently appeared nearby. He wasn't all that worried about being busted for serving kids, knowing that the neighborhood cops would do nothing but give him a warning. No, it was pouring more rotgut into Whitey that worried him. One or two more and Marie would be missing a grandparent at the communion.

"Let's go, Gramps," pleaded Jack, "Mama's gonna kill us both."

"Sonny, I'll not have ya disrespect your elders. Now put your keister down there, and drink what's set before ya, and say thanks to Almighty God that made this glorious day."

The burn Jack felt when the whiskey hit his throat was a sensation he never forgot. Years later, when he had the lead at AA meetings, he not only described that hair-raising, gut-wrenching feeling, but he'd swear his body had perfect recall of it as well. When he puked on the tree lawn walking home with his very drunk grandfather more than an hour later, he swore he'd never touch the stuff again.

That was forty years ago: forty years of binges, of drunk tanks all over the country, of stints in the county work-house and a dresser full of DUIs. It was also twenty years of promises—to himself, to his mother, and to a long string of girlfriends. Twenty years of meetings, of holding hands with a bunch of sweaty strangers, of talking bullshit for their benefit and thinking only of a stiff Johnnie Walker while they recited the Lord's Prayer.

What a joke, he thought, as he stared at himself in the unframed mirror. *The closest I ever came to "serenity" was when I was passed out and didn't feel the big hole in my middle, the one that ached for the first hit in the morning.*

"Well, that was all peanuts, small-time stuff," he crooned to his image as he tried to steady his hand with the straight blade, which was making unexpected bolts across his chin. As he reached for a piece of toilet paper to stick on the cut blossoming into a bud of red to the left of his mouth, he thought about his current situation and about his AA sponsor's words of advice: "Repentance won't do it this time, buddy. Vehicular homicide is damned serious stuff, and we're talking about killing a kid to boot. Whatever they offer you, even if it's eight to fifteen years in the slammer, I wouldn't go to trial on this one." Jack had taken his words to heart, since he knew that his sponsor just happened to be one of the best defense lawyers in the county.

What Jack hadn't shared with his sponsor was the fact that he had the proverbial "friend at court" and this case was going to plead, all right, but without any jail time at all.

|3|

WHEN CASEY BEGAN reading the file in the Diemert case, she was surprised by the amount of tragedy the victim's family had already experienced prior to their daughter's death. She was also struck by how easily appearances could deceive the casual observer. The State Attorney's notes were thorough, detailed and dispelled any notion Casey had about the privileged lives of the very rich. The interviews with the victim's parents contained personal and sometimes disturbing insights into their family and the what lay beneath the facade of suburban ease and comfort.

The first ten years of Amy Cohen's childhood read like a fairy tale. She lived with her brother and parents in a beautiful suburb of Detroit. She had some friends from the private school she attended, and despite her distinct overbite, she was not unattractive.

Although she was a mediocre student, her teachers in grade school were more concerned about her lack of maturity and social awkwardness. Nevertheless, she passed from grade to grade, and everyone assumed that given her father's tremendous wealth and stature, Amy would marry early and well and take an advanced degree in country club living.

Her father, Harold, was raised in far different circumstances. His childhood home had been in one of the poorest sections of downtown Detroit. He was an only child, imprisoned in a small apartment with a single window that looked down on a dark stucco courtyard. At precisely 3:45 pm each day, a thin arrow of light would lay itself across the rose-and-vine patterned living room rug. Harold Cohen was determined to extend the half-life of this meager illumination and, without realizing it, became an expert in the physical properties of light transportation.

Thirty years later, with a doctorate from Case Institute of Technology in Cleveland and a patent on the trajectory of indirect headlamps used on Cavalier cars, Harold was one of the wealthiest auto executives in the world. He had everything. Apparently.

He had married well, a fact that was a source of more pleasure to his parents than his early and enviable financial success. His wife, Miriam, thought of herself as a good enough wife. She cooked what was in fashion at any given time, volunteered at the synagogue when it meshed with her schedule for the beauty shop and carpool, and did her wifely duties in the bedroom with all the enthusiasm most people bring to a dentist appointment. She was also, without question, a devoted mother.

She had long ago accepted that her husband was a workaholic, gone every day but the Sabbath and many evenings as well. Climbing the corporate ladder, even for a brilliant engineer with a priceless patent, required long hours of work and socializing. Nevertheless, Miriam was content with a life that was not much different than the lives of her friends. And she had the pleasure of raising her two wonderful children.

She would say later that God ripped the joy from her heart with the skill and precision of a cardiac surgeon.

The day after Michael's twelfth birthday, he and a friend were blindsided by a pickup truck driven by a seventeen-year-old who Harold would forever insist was high on drugs. No drugs were ever found, and the driver tested negative for alcohol. Michael was killed instantly. The other child lingered for weeks. The driver of the truck was never charged and a civil lawsuit for damages against him was dismissed for lack of evidence. Harold Cohen was profoundly bitter about the failures of the police investigation and the justice system, and he vowed to redress that injustice in some way, somehow, someday.

Amy, who was barely ten years old when Michael died, felt the world tilt. She and Michael had merely tolerated each other publicly, but in private she worshipped her older brother. The steady parade of friends and family at their home following the funeral did nothing for her. The weight of her loss seemed to impress no one and, not surprisingly, her grief for her lost brother turned into vapor next to the monumental mourning of her parents. Her parents were inconsolable. They went to the synagogue every day, morning and evening. Miriam hardly left her room otherwise. No one noticed that Amy Cohen had slipped away into her own world, one where she was somebody other than the dead boy's younger sister.

Twenty years later, just when there didn't seem to be any possible mourning left in this world, Harold and Miriam Cohen sat in the West Palm Beach coroner's office and heard him describe the gruesome facts of their daughter Amy's death.

Harold's initial reaction was disbelief. Although Amy had been estranged from the family for years, Harold and Miriam had kept track of her through some of her friends who periodically called with news or sightings. Amy's problems with drugs and alcohol were nothing new, but by all accounts she was living in south Florida with a man who held a steady job. They had been lulled into a false hope that life for their daughter, although a long way from what they had hoped and planned for her, was headed toward stability.

That hope, they told the State Attorney, had been shattered when they opened the front page of the *Detroit Free Press* several months ago. The details of their daughter's death were scant, but the sensational parts of the story were laid out in graphic detail. Everyone familiar with the case had initially assumed that Amy's death was a bizarre and horrendous accident. Some news wags compared it to circus trainers who had been gored or attacked by animals they considered loving pets.

Now, as Amy's parents sat with the coroner and a member of the Palm Beach County State Attorney's office, they began to understand that this was no freak accident. The windowless room in which they sat hearing, for the first time, the precise details of the manner of their daughter's death seemed as colorless and cold as the face and voice of the coroner.

But it was the interjection by the State Attorney that would alter in some fundamental way whatever was left of Harold and Miriam's lives and peace of mind. "We don't believe that this was an accident. Considerable evidence points to an intentional act or acts by your daughter's roommate . . ." Charles Graham looked down at his notes. "er, common-law husband. I'm here today because our office is asking the coroner, in light of our investigation, to rule that your daughter's death was a homicide."

Graham looked at the Coroner. Miriam looked at the floor, almost casually watching tears travel from her chin to her hands folded neatly on her lap. Harold looked at Miriam, his face distorted and deeply colored in hues of red and purple.

The official report and history had ended there and Casey could only wonder what had gone through Harold Cohen's mind, what angst and pain he must have endured to lose another child to another act of violence.

Many months later, Casey would know, along with everyone else who followed the case, what had been Harold Cohen's first thought that horrible afternoon with the coroner. This time, he vowed silently, this time, his child's killer would not go unpunished.

4

THE JUDGES, ALONG with their clerks and bailiffs, were
slowly finding seats in Judge Spellman's courtroom. A few
people sat down in what was normally the jury box, but
most took seats in the rows behind the bar that separated the
public and press from the courtroom itself. The carpet had
been replaced several times in this and the other courtrooms,
but much to everyone's dismay, an institutional smell still
clung to the air. New jurors noticed it immediately, although
if they suffered through very long trials, they claimed that
they became impervious to it. No juror, however, became
immune to the dizzying sensation produced by the gridded
wood paneling on the wall opposite the jury box. Some
judges had attempted to lessen the hypnotic effect of the

wall by hanging rugs or other artifacts. These decorations were "liberated" on such a regular basis, however, that the judges were reduced to simply admonishing new jurors to avoid looking at the wall.

Casey took a seat at the back of the courtroom, hoping that she could slide out early to start her weekend. She needed a break; they all did. She had originally planned to visit her parents at their home in Winter Park, just outside Orlando. But after the chaos of the last few days, she chose a quiet evening close to home instead. She would walk the beach in MacArthur Park, have a bite at the Tiki Hut on Singer Island, and turn in early with her Sleepytime Tea. If that all seemed horribly boring and old, it touched some primal need in her to be closer to nature and home and leave the fear of the last several days as far behind her as possible.

Her daydream was cut short by an abrupt bump and a deep voice that announced, "Since this seems to be the row attracting the best-looking staff at the court, there must be room for one more." Luke Anderson sat down just far enough from Casey that the flirtatiousness of his comment would not provoke a snide remark from her. Casey was in a good mood, thinking about her weekend, so she merely gave the Police Chief an engaging smile and shifted her gaze to the front of the room where Judge Spellman was banging a glass with a pencil in a fruitless effort to get people to stop talking.

"Please, folks, please. I know you're all anxious to get out of here. This meeting will be brief. Since the courthouses will be open for business as usual on Monday morning, I want to caution everyone about making assumptions regarding what has happened and what could happen. To assume that the bombing two days ago was an isolated incident would be foolish. To assume that the perpetrators have any connection to the homicide case in Judge Kanterman's courtroom would be unfair. And to assume that we can prevent another incident would be downright dangerous. So I want each of you to look around you, connect with the people closest to you, and form a protective bond with your co-workers."

Before Casey could look at Luke's face, she felt his breath on her ear and cheek. "It won't take much to bond with you, Miss Casey." Luke's lips were so close that she thought if she turned her head slightly, they'd be welded, not bonded. Instead, she forced herself to keep her gaze on the front of courtroom while she watched Judge Spellman's lips moving but heard nothing because of the pounding in her ears as her blood pressure and her imagination soared. When she saw Judge Kanterman stand and move toward her, Casey was sure that her sexual fantasies had been obvious to everyone, and she sat back abruptly against the bench. But the judge walked past Casey and stopped beside Ben, who was seated just one row back. Not meaning to intrude, Casey couldn't help but overhear the judge.

"Say, Ben, I wonder if you could stop by Monday. I saw a copy of the journal entry on the hit-and-run case where the driver killed a young girl. I thought the case had been moved to my docket since Judge Clarke was in Tallahassee, but I guess she found the time to take a plea and impose sentence in the case. I'd like to clear it off my docket. Have a good weekend."

As Judge Spellman continued his lecture about courthouse safety, Casey noticed Ben slip out of his seat and head toward the doors. *Probably going to take care of whatever Judge Kanterman asked him about,* she thought. *What a good bailiff my friend has become.* Casey shifted in her seat, anxious for the meeting to end so she could begin her weekend.

As always, Janet Kanterman took the stairs to the parking level. She was a creature of habit and ate the same thing for breakfast every day (yogurt and raisin bread toast), drove the same make of car (Toyota Camry), and parked in the same spot in the underground garage at the Justice

Complex. Unlike many of her colleagues who preferred the prime parking places next to the door to the courthouse, Janet liked to protect the anonymity of her car, its contents, and what it might say about its owner and driver. Consequently, she parked in the spot farthest from the elevators. Tonight, as always, she would perform the ritual of opening her car doors with her key, then releasing her trunk in order to stow her briefcase and any materials she wanted to assure would be secure.

As she left the parking garage, Janet thought briefly about some threatening letters she had received recently, all but one in reference to the dog case. Perhaps she would talk to the court administrator about changing her parking place for the duration of this case. Contrary to what some of her colleagues believed, she would actually welcome a plea bargain in the dog case, one that would avoid a trial that she estimated would take weeks of her time. In fact, it was the team of defense lawyers who continued to balk at any notion of a plea. After all, they argued, the State had made the decision to prosecute this case as an intentional murder when the evidence most clearly supported a trial for manslaughter, the legal term for a crime of passion. It would be the State's burden to sell a jury on a first-degree murder charge—and the defense team was confident that it couldn't be done.

Therefore, defense counsel reasoned, so long as the State insisted on going for broke, the interests of their client were best served by letting the State do just that. This wouldn't be the first time that prosecutors over-indicted and it surely wouldn't be the last. It simply produced more defense verdicts at trial than anyone cared to talk about. And beyond the judge pointing out to both sides that many seemingly straightforward trials took on a life of their own and it was damned unpredictable what course that life would take, there wasn't a thing she could do to break the logjam.

|5|

THE STATE ATTORNEY'S office is located in a building less than fifty yards from the main courthouse, and despite the widespread and not entirely unwarranted perception that the state's lawyers (often referred to as prosecutors) get special treatment from the judges and have a quantum edge over the defense bar, their offices don't reflect their power. Everyone in the criminal justice system understands that prosecutors are either heroes or villains in the eyes of the public, depending on who is being tried and for what crime. But within the confines of their offices, they are often idealistic and dedicated men and women searching for the perfect balance between their roles as champions of the state's laws and guardians of the state's constitution, including the rights of the individual.

The larger area of the offices is divided into cubicles, and it is only the chief of the division, the elected State Attorney, who is given some real privacy, and even that isn't very much. Still, Charlie Graham was grateful for whatever he got. He was a tall, slim man with an engaging mind, a youthful appearance, and a natural theatrical talent. He had honed his dramatic skills at the Yale Pudding Clubs, where he also collected East Coast contacts that suited his ambitions, which went well beyond the confines of this court. In anticipation of a lot of upcoming TV and press coverage in the *State of Florida v. Josiah Diemert* case, his wife was busily shopping at the Hugo Boss outlet for new suits.

Charlie was feeling pretty pumped. He was relieved that the vehicular homicide in front of Judge Clarke was undoubtedly going to plead and get shipped for mega time. He had every confidence that a dead kid and a drunk scumbag like Jack McGinty would be a slam-dunk for the state.

That was true despite the fact that Lloyd Schwartzman, the guardian angel of the addicted and alcoholic in West Palm Beach, represented the jerk, and Lloyd was a hell of a good lawyer. But even Lloyd couldn't keep this one out of jail. He'd seen pictures of the kid lying in the street, and if the law had allowed him, Charlie Graham would have pushed for a death sentence for this scumbag.

On the brighter side, he mused as he gathered his pile of court files to carry across the street for the first of what would likely be many hearings, the attorneys on the dog case were ready to begin discussions about seating a jury and managing the press. The only potential hurdle Charlie faced in that case was a very idealistic judge. He would not soon forget Janet Kanterman's rejoinder when he had chided her about the courteous treatment she accorded defendants.

"How else would you address an innocent man, Mr. Prosecutor?" she'd inquired. Given that bleeding-heart attitude, he doubted she would work with him to get a manslaughter plea in the dog case. And if the truth were told, that was probably the only charge he could get a conviction for—certainly not the intentional murder his office had insisted on prosecuting.

Mind you, he reasoned, it was standard practice to ask for more and prepare for less. If you waited to have hard facts and evidence to support every case brought by the state, you would never get the plea bargains that were the meat and potatoes of the system. They all knew that meant that a few chumps would plead to a lesser charge because their court-appointed defense lawyer convinced them that it was better than taking a chance that they might get a bad jury and end up spending the rest of their lives in jail. They copped a plea even if they weren't guilty of a damn thing, because nothing good had ever happened in their crappy lives and nothing, they believed, ever would.

If that was cynical, Charlie had long ago made peace with the notion that there was collateral damage in the pursuit of justice, just as there was in any other war.

Charlie pushed the button on the elevator and felt a surge of relief that the morning crowds had thinned. Many courthouses permitted prosecutors to use the elevators reserved for judges. Charlie was no snob, but on more than one occasion he had found himself riding with a defendant and his family. It was an awkward situation and potentially dangerous. He straightened his shoulders as he caught sight of himself in the elevator mirror. His mother's admonition still rang in his mind: "Stand tall, Charlie, and always look like you believe in what you're doing." He would have added, "Even if you don't."

|6|

WHEN THE NEW courthouse was built in 1994, everyone was confident not only that it was modern in every sense of the word, but also that it would have the same lasting stature and importance as the Old Courthouse, a landmark historical building that was now one of the premier tourist attractions in West Palm Beach.

As Judge Barbara Clarke was so fond of saying (someone had done it in needlepoint, and it hung on the wall in her chambers), "Whenever you assume something is true without checking the facts, you'll be wrong 78 percent of the time." Barbara was reminded of that maxim as she stepped over the debris still lying in piles around the corners of the Justice Complex's first floor. The maintenance people had done a good job of sweeping up the plaster and trash that fell in the blast's aftermath, but the incongruity of the debris and the richly colored marble floor and pillars only added to her unease. Clearly, the new building was as vulnerable as any other, and it was folly to assume otherwise.

Barbara decided to walk the perimeter of the first several floors before she headed for the private elevator to her courtroom. Her strict fitness regimen had helped her maintain her naturally athletic figure, a real contrast to most of the women in her family. She was aware that diabetes was rampant in the African-American community, and she was determined to literally outrun it. When she reached the floor she shared with Judge Kanterman and several other judges, she was relieved to find that things were very much in order. The hallways outside the courtrooms, an area where assistant prosecutors, defense lawyers, and staff hung out and swapped everything from plea deals to sports stats, were empty.

She was surprised to find her bailiff working at his computer. As she approached his desk, she quietly said, "Hey," hoping not to frighten him. It had the opposite effect, and all six-plus lanky feet of him jerked so forcefully out of his chair that he had to grab the desk's edge to avoid landing on the floor.

"Easy, Ben," Judge Clarke said as she grabbed for him. "I didn't mean to startle you. Frankly, I didn't expect to find you or anyone at work this late. I came here straight from the court in Tallahassee."

Ben was still gasping for breath as he turned toward the judge. He towered over her, as he did over everyone. It struck Judge Clarke, as she looked up at his thin, angular face, that he seemed as agitated as he was surprised.

"Are you all right? You seem really shaken."

"Sorry, Your Honor, but you know, with everything that's happened, it's, like, creepy around here."

"Well, I appreciate your diligence. It helps to know that someone is minding the store when you're out of town." She tried to look past him at the computer screen, but Ben had moved quickly to block her view. Barbara was amused, assuming he was using the computer for personal business, a practice clearly forbidden but tolerated by most judges. She knew next to nothing about Ben's personal life. She had hired him from a pool of applicants sent by the court administrator. She was aware that he had taken a leave of absence from law school in Boca Raton after an accident that shattered his knee and required multiple surgeries. She was happy to help.

"Just catching up on journal entries, Judge. I know how you dislike having a tall stack of orders to sign, especially when you've been gone for a while." Ben hit the computer's power button as he was talking and grabbed for his jacket hanging on the back of the swivel chair. "We can go over these tomorrow, if you'd prefer. Judge Spellman canceled all our trials until Monday, so there are only pretrials and pleas set for the next few days." His last words were almost inaudible to Barbara. He was out the door, and she was headed toward her chambers, feeling uneasy about her exchange with him. She shrugged her shoulders as if to dismiss this additional and unwanted intrusion on her thoughts.

She had accepted the offer to sit with the Court of Appeals in Tallahassee with enthusiasm, partly because it was a change of scene, partly because it was an honor to be asked, and partly because she needed a little time away from her husband. She knew it was long past time to make a decision about her failed marriage, but she continued to be trapped by her own fantasies of marital resurrection as well as her personal disapproval of divorce as an option. Her daily struggle to focus her attention on her work and not on her domestic woes had taken a toll on her. When she had received the invitation to go to Tallahassee, she had seen it as a temporary reprieve and jumped at the chance.

Still, everything had its price. In this instance, she had been forced to ask other judges to pick up a lot of her criminal docket, to take criminal pleas for her, and to sign journal entries when Ben had cleared them with her. In truth, she had leaned a lot on Ben. He was like a junior judge at this point. She wondered briefly if the pressure had been too much for him.

Judge Clarke closed the door to her chambers and, for the first time in her career, turned the lock.

Outside the door, Ben heard the click of the lock in the hallway, where he stood outside the judge's line of sight. He stepped quietly back into the antechamber. Reaching across his desk, he found the CD slot on the side of his computer, removed the disc, scribbled "JM" on the center, and placed it in his pencil drawer, a drawer that he could and did lock before leaving. It was only when he hit the street that he had misgivings about the location of the disc. He shook those off as he headed for Clematis Street, where he was now a minor celebrity for surviving a bomb attack.

7

CASEY HAD LOST her virginity just three days after her sixteenth birthday. She had not expected anything so monumental to happen with so little fanfare. She had discussed sex with no one, and most of her information came from the boy who was now sulking about her unwillingness to "help him out." Since she knew so little about the act itself, she had no expectations regarding helping herself out. Over the succeeding months, she learned through talking with her girlfriends that the appeasement of young boys with grown men's appetites was an unpleasant reality for many young girls anxious to please and unwilling to put that thing in their mouth.

She didn't have sex again until her senior year in high

school, but this time she thought she was in love, and she was sure that all the talks and all the magazine articles she'd read had her a lot better prepared to get something out of the experience. When it was no more satisfying on either a physical or emotional level than the first time (except that this time it was on a mattress in the boy's basement, instead of the back seat of a car), she figured there was something wrong with her or the whole thing was just overrated.

Time and some good partners had changed her views and her feelings about sex. But the encounters had been sporadic, and she feared that she might be one of those women who never achieved orgasm, at least not one they wanted to talk about.

Those early experiences had definitely not prepared her for the present encounter. At this moment her breath was so labored that she was certain she was going to pass out or have a stroke.

As her eyes opened in amazement, Luke's head popped up just above her pelvic bone. "Has Madam had enough of the appetizer? Would Madam like the main course?"

"Yes, yes, please, Luke, please give Madam the main course," she cried out, laughing between gasps. With that he rose up over her, spread her legs with an urgency that seemed almost brutal, and then calmly and slowly slid inside her.

This is like a roller coaster, she thought, as her body rose up one side of her pleasure and came roaring down the other. The sensations changed as he grew bigger inside her, and she sensed him approaching the crest of his own ride. "Wait for me!" she demanded, feeling now like the caboose on a runaway train. He waited; he slowed for just an instant until she caught up, and then he drove them both home. She screamed with pleasure.

When her breathing finally slowed, she shook her head to clear it in the afterglow of euphoria. To her dismay, Luke took her movement as a signal of discomfort and rolled off her. Neither one spoke, both of them huffing and clearly feeling awkward at the intensity of the coupling and their surprise that it had happened at all.

"Tell me you didn't plan all this?" Casey asked coquettishly as she turned toward him.

The grin that spread across Luke's face and up to his ears gave a hint as to his answer. "Not all of it, for sure. Even I, with as rich a sexual fantasy life as you'll find north of the Everglades, could not have imagined this."

Casey flipped to her other side. She was hurt by his answer. A rich sexual fantasy life, indeed! When she had responded to Luke's awkward attempts at small talk after the judge's meeting ended, she was delighted by his invitation to meet her for drinks on the beach. She knew that Luke was the subject of courthouse gossip, especially because he had been through a messy divorce and yet seemed to live a quiet, almost reclusive life. Casey had to admit that she was intrigued. She was coming dangerously close to a certain age, as her mother liked to describe it, and although Luke might be considered a little old for her, he was a very sexy and apparently eligible man. When she agreed to meet him, the cynicism she had acquired working in the courthouse should have kicked into gear. But it didn't. What did kick in was her wish for male company, her wish not to spend the weekend completely alone, and, let's face it, her wish to know Luke better. Now she felt like a fool, and her body language did nothing to disguise her displeasure.

"Hey, hey, Miss Casey." His big hairy arm came across her, and he moved her face gently to look into his. "That was meant as a supreme compliment. My god, woman, weren't you as amazed as I was? Sure, I planned to have a nice dinner. Sure, I hoped for a little romance, maybe even a friendly encounter in the sack, but nothing like this! I am certifiably smitten, girl."

And I'm grateful not to be a one-night stand—especially with this guy, thought Casey as she turned to face him, feeling his small forests of chest hair brush against her nipples and realizing that the evening was far from over. Her breath quickened again as she felt his erection literally spring against her thigh. God, she wished she could text her best friend about the miracle. But as agile as she was proving to be in the sack, even she couldn't manage that one.

8

JACK MCGINTY LIKED to volunteer to do the coffee at meetings, partly to relieve the boredom, but mostly because he could occasionally get someone to sign his court papers early, proving his attendance before the meeting began so that he could cut out when the need arose. He wasn't about to complain, mind you. Six weeks of AA meetings as a sentence for vehicular homicide was—well, it was goddamned unbelievable! So unbelievable that Jack hadn't mentioned a word about it to anyone at the meetings he attended. Actually, the only time it really bothered him was when the meetings were held in the kitchen at St. Helen's Church. Every once in a while his eyes would close during the reading of the "Promises," and he'd see the top of that little girl's head as it slid up the hood of his car before sailing off the side and onto the street. He'd have to choke back a sob and make it sound like a belch.

He tried to stay away from the church meetings. Those evenings made him run like a man possessed to the nearest bar, where he'd remain until closing time or until he was tossed out. One thing was for sure—a rule he never compromised on. He never went to a meeting sloshed. Damn, it pissed him off when he'd see other guys come in staggering a little and blowing their dragon breath all over everybody. And that was invariably the bozo who wanted to share his story, except the dude made absolutely no sense. Some of the guys thought it was funny, but Jack McGinty disapproved. You had to draw the line somewhere.

As he sat, half listening to some old lady telling them the story of her early drinking days and sounding like she really missed those days, vomit and all, his mind wandered to his next trip to Key West. There would be a large shipment waiting for him, and some of his best customers were getting restless for their stuff. He never could understand how these people got hooked on stuff like Vicodin or Oxy-whatever-it's-called. But hooked they were, and some of his benefactors, folks who had helped him sort out his current mess with the law, were among his prime users. And Jesus, that prescription shit was expensive! The part he really didn't get was that you took your stuff alone, so there wasn't even the short-lived social life you got when you were a drunk. And booze, even in the quantities that he drank it, was not only less expensive, it was legal.

He was anxious to leave, but he knew enough people by now that if he ducked out early, he'd sure as shit get a call from one of them before the night ended. Some of these guys spent a good part of every day on this do-gooder stuff, even the guys who'd been clean for decades. "Well," he muttered, chuckling to himself, "it just isn't my cup of tea."

Jack left early and headed home for a short nap. He and his partner should be on the road early tomorrow morning. With skillful driving, a clean hookup with their friends at dockside, and sparse traffic on I-95, they'd make the turnaround in a day. He felt a real sense of urgency this trip. There was one customer in particular that he didn't want to piss off.

9

A MURDER TRIAL is different from any other. That is true everywhere, but especially in Florida, where every charge of murder carries a possible death sentence unless the prosecutor decides to settle for life in prison. Not surprisingly, therefore, the rules for the admission of evidence are strict, especially for testimony that is not from an eyewitness, a rarity in murder cases, since the victim is usually not available, and if there are credible live witnesses to the crime, there is almost always a plea by the defendant. Most criminal trials and all murder cases are inherently more dramatic than any civil trial could ever hope to be. The trial for damages against O.J. Simpson may be one of the few exceptions to that rule.

Because the stakes are high and both sides are looking

for that Perry Mason surprise witness to appear at the last minute, these trials are also unpredictable. Everyone involved in the criminal process knows it, feels it, and even smells it. Early in the pretrial stage of an exciting case, the courtroom is crowded with lawyers, court reporters, deputy sheriffs, and bored court personnel with time on their hands and an excess of curiosity. As the trial date nears, the case draws more and more attention, and people begin to express opinions, and occasionally lay a wager on when a plea bargain will be struck between the state and the defendant, and what the bargain is going to look like.

The State of Florida v. Josiah Diemert was going right down to the wire. Secretaries hung around the elevators, hoping to catch a glimpse of some of the national media covering the case. The halls were crowded with crews hefting large cameras on their shoulders and trying to look like media stars themselves. Inside Judge Kanterman's courtroom, the defense team was huddled around the table, leafing through large notebooks of evidence. Behind the bar that separated the spectators from the court personnel and the jury box, a few witnesses had been permitted by the deputy sheriffs to take seats before the jury selection began. Once the trial commenced, anyone who might possibly testify was barred from the courtroom.

The defense team was headed by Lloyd Schwartzman. He was highly regarded in the West Palm Beach community and generally well liked by lawyers and judges. His work assisting substance abusers was well known, but his charitable works also extended to raising funds for the homeless, working for the local Kiwanis Club's Peanut Day, and many more programs that benefited the poor and disenfranchised. When the Miami lawyers who represented Josiah Diemert were granted a change of venue, they knew they needed respected local counsel who would work for court appointed fees, and it took no time at all to find and hire Schwartzman.

At this moment, however, Schwartzman had a huge problem. He couldn't stand his client. In Lloyd's view, the little son of a bitch should be dropped down an elevator shaft. Not that he believed that Amy Cohen's brutal death was intentional murder; in fact, he was convinced that both Josiah and Amy were so drunk and wasted on that terrible night that neither of them felt or understood much of what happened. Rather, it was the fact that this jerk was showing up for every pretrial barely coherent and had arrived for trial a few minutes ago so clearly stoned, on God knew what, that Lloyd was seriously considering a request for a continuance based on the defendant's constitutional right to be present at the trial of his case.

The door to the judge's chambers swung open, and her bailiff, Casey, called over to Lloyd, "Mr. Schwartzman, I understand that Charlie Graham and the other assistant prosecutors are here, and the judge would like to meet with all counsel to lay down some ground rules for the trial. Please come on back whenever you're able."

Lloyd Schwartzman turned to the team of lawyers from Miami and practically spit out, "See if you can get this bum sobered up before we begin jury selection. I don't know what happens down south, but up here there's a problem when the defendant in a murder trial is nodding off at the defense table." Schwartzman turned heel and, without even the courtesy of inviting the out-of-town lead counsel to follow him, strode across the courtroom to meet with Judge Kanterman and the prosecution team. He was in a foul mood, he knew, but he had no idea how foul things might become.

10

JUDGE KANTERMAN'S CHAMBERS were breathtakingly neat. Although stacks of journal entries and draft opinions decorated every space on the room's window shelves, the judge's massive wooden desk was completely clean of papers and clutter. Charlie Graham was especially impressed since he knew she had been handling a considerable portion of Judge Clarke's docket while Judge Clarke sat in with the appeals court. He was also surprised since he had never considered Kanterman a precise thinker. The opinions that issued from her courtroom tended to have as much social commentary as legal analysis. His thoughts were interrupted by the arrival of the judge with her bailiff, Casey, on her heels. Despite the discrepancy in height, the much shorter judge had an undeniable presence, and the respect she evoked was clear when everyone stood at her approach.

"Thank you, gentlemen, for your prompt arrival. Before we begin the process of seating the jury in this case, I need to rule on some important issues. First, at no time will the dog be brought into the courtroom. That motion was made by the defense counsel, and I am granting the request on the obvious ground that jurors might be so intimidated by the presence of the animal that their ability to fairly judge the case would be impaired."

Charlie Graham stood, although it was really not necessary to do so in the judge's chambers.

"Your Honor, with all due respect, our objections to that line of reasoning are based on common sense. Granted, this is an unusual case where the co-defendant is a pit bull, not another person. Nevertheless, in every homicide case where the co-defendant is available, and no matter how gruesome the crime, the jury is permitted to see and take the measure of all the parties to the crime in question. We fail to see why this case should be different."

Schwartzman was out of his chair before Graham was back in his.

"Let's put this to rest. I thought we had, but Mr. Graham is following his usual practice of being a "legal pit bull" and hanging on until he gets his decision or asks for this court to send the question upstairs to the appellate court before we can proceed. It is patently absurd to suggest that this dog be treated as a co-defendant. This confused animal will be further traumatized by the prosecution's effort to parade him, muzzled and leashed, before a jury. It is tantamount to abuse of the animal and, in my mind, of the jurors as well."

"I've issued my ruling, and it stands. Furthermore, I do not believe that it warrants an immediate referral to the Court of Appeals. It may be grounds for appeal at some later date, but not at this point. All right, gentlemen, what else must be addressed by this court prior to turning our attention to seating a jury?"

Lloyd Schwartzman shot a glance over at Charlie Graham and raised his eyebrows. Charlie nodded and rose. "Judge, we have a problem with one of our key witnesses. The state plans to prove that Butch was trained to attack and that the defendant was his sole trainer. That relationship between a pit bull and his trainer is pivotal to our case. We plan to call a number of experts to opine generally on this phenomenon, but we have enlisted the services of a local dog trainer to study Butch's behavior at length and to testify to his character and his devotion to Josiah Diemert, the defendant in this case."

"Yes, yes, I'm fully briefed on this issue, Mr. Graham. I don't mean to rush you, but I have a throbbing headache, and we have much to accomplish before we break." In fact, Janet had been suffering from constant headaches and abdominal pain for the past week. She promised herself she would visit her doctor over the weekend if the pain continued.

"I apologize, Your Honor. Our problem is simply the . . . uh, attitude and style of this witness. This dog trainer operates a school for puppies and problem dogs. She refers to herself as the Puppy Priestess, and her school is called Parochial School for Wayward Puppies. As the court might suspect, our witness is quite flamboyant and insists on being addressed as Ms. Priestess. She also refuses to testify in anything other than pink sweats that bear the name of her business, the phone number, and her e-mail address."

"Oh, my," Judge Kanterman sighed audibly while she struggled not to smile. It was a rare sight when the State Attorney, and especially one as powerful as Charlie Graham, had a witness control problem. And with a witness who insisted on appearing in pink sweats! "Just what is it you're asking the court to do with this witness, Mr. Graham? We can't bring in the fashion police."

"Now, that's not exactly fair, Judge. We regularly impose dress restrictions on witnesses. We won't allow see-through tank tops or short shorts. Why should a walking billboard be permitted to sit on the witness stand? We simply want the court to admonish the witness that the use of the courtroom to advertise businesses or services is prohibited."

"I'd like to help you out, Charlie, but I'm afraid the Constitution won't let me set a prior restraint on someone's right of free speech. Whether we like it or not, until your witness shows up in the sort of gear you've described and it is found offensive to the process or the jury, there's not a darn thing you or I can do about it." The pain Janet had referred to earlier had intensified and now slid rapidly across her right temple and took up residence in and above her left eye. She stood as a signal to everyone that the conference was done.

"We'll break here and reconvene at one this afternoon to begin the jury selection process."

As the lawyers moved toward the door, chatting amongst themselves, Casey moved to the head of the group "Hey, guys, she's really not feeling well, and you know jury selection can take forever. Also, because this trial could take weeks, we'll need at least a half-dozen alternates to sit with the dozen regular jurors. So to make it a little easier on everyone, the judge would like you to submit the questions you plan to ask prospective jurors beyond the standard ones about education, family, et cetera. Bring them with you this afternoon, and be sure you have a copy for each side as well as the court."

Just as Lloyd Schwartzman's back was disappearing through her chamber doors, Judge Kanterman called out to him, "Say, Lloyd, didn't you represent the vehicular homicide case that entered a plea? I'm still trying to sort things out about that case."

Schwartzman turned around and, looking nervously at the judge and Casey, replied," I'm embarrassed to say I was so busy that I asked Ben Toledo to find a public defender to take care of the sentencing. I'll check on it and get back to you ladies."

Lloyd was doubly fortunate that day: first because he didn't see the look that passed between the judge and Casey over his use of the term "ladies," as though they were at a tea party, and second because he knew that handing off the sentencing in a case where a child had been killed by a drunk driver could give him major grief with the bar association. He was relieved, nonetheless, by the fact that his client Jack McGinty had enthusiastically signed a waiver to allow Lloyd to withdraw as his attorney and to substitute a public defender. In fact, if he recalled correctly, it had been McGinty himself who had suggested the switch.

|11|

JUDGE BARBARA CLARKE stared out the window of her chambers at a flock of blackbirds perched on the portico of the library. As she watched, the birds peeled off in pairs and threesomes. No single bird acted alone. *We're all like that,* she thought. *We like to do things, to take risks, but we prefer to do it with others like us.* She shook her head to bring her mind out of her reverie. It was more than reverie, she realized. It was melancholy. *No,* she chided herself, *face up to it, sweetie. They call this depression.* She abruptly swiveled her chair so that she faced the wall of books opposite the windows. Knowing full well the cause of her depression, knowing that there was no acceptable solution to restore her to her former sense of well-being, she nevertheless clung to her hope for a miracle.

She believed in miracles. Her childhood on the South Side of Chicago had given her no reason to hope for anything beyond a menial job like her mother's—cleaning houses or doing laundry for rich white women in the suburbs. Her inconsistent performance in elementary school, coupled with a string of reprimands for skipping school, made even those jobs look like a reach. All that had changed in her first year of high school. Her mother scratched together enough money to pay tuition at a nearby parish parochial school. Barbara showed up on opening day in her new uniform and with freshly braided cornrows glistening like a prairie in Kansas on a sunny day. It took less than two minutes and her first (and last) run-in with the mother superior to understand that these people meant business. The next six years were a blur of books, tests, awards (both academic and athletic), and a free ride to Northwestern University for her undergraduate studies. If she thought about her race, what her mother still referred to as being "colored," it was only to compare her sleek and well-muscled body to those of the chubby white girls who were determined to play basketball as a weight-loss program.

She had relished, however, becoming the first black woman on law review at the University of Michigan's prestigious law school. Although she could not secure one of the prized rooms in the Law Quad, she had her own space at the law review offices and in the reading room of the magnificent Tudor-style Law Library. Barbara knew that some of her classmates regarded her as nothing more than a poster child for affirmative action, a by-product of the generally despised decision in the *Bakke* case. But Barbara knew better. She not only worked harder (and played less) than other students, but she also had a near-photographic memory. The combination kept her at the top of her class in undergraduate school and at the law school as well.

But work and brains didn't leave much opportunity for socializing, especially for a tall and, she admitted to herself, rather ordinary-looking woman. No wonder she fell like the proverbial ton of bricks when Ellison Gabriel Watson stumbled into her life and then consumed it.

Ellison Watson was on a basketball scholarship at Michigan, and although he was only a junior, he was nearly twenty-three years old when they met. Barbara was sipping coffee from Drakes Candy Shoppe near Hill Auditorium and waiting for the shuttle to take her to the new student housing at North Campus. Ellis, huffing, puffing, and smelling strongly of sweat, collapsed on the bench beside her.

"Damn!" he muttered, looking at the stopwatch on his wrist. "Shit!"

Barbara turned toward him with what she hoped was a withering look. Instead, she stared at the most handsome man she had ever seen. He stared back for a moment and then bent down to tie a wandering shoelace.

"Sorry, sorry, sorry. I'm just disgusted with myself." His head was wagging back and forth, and he dropped it below his knees. "Look. You are probably one of those fabulously built black girls who never bothered to use their God-given physical talent to play a sport. So if . . ."

"Excuse me!" Barbara nearly spat at him. "First of all, I'm a woman, not a girl. Second, what would a white boy like you know about black bodies in the first place?"

His index finger was dancing in the air. "Whoops. I think you already had a *first,* and you're wrong, lady—or should I say woman? I'd be willing to bet that I've got as many black ancestors as you have, and who are you to be calling names?"

The hard and insistent knocking on her chamber door broke Barbara's reverie. She wouldn't be able to revisit the courtship, the wedding, or the honeymoon on Grand Cayman. That was too bad. Those were amazing memories. Ellis, as he preferred to be called, made sex seem like an Olympic sport. She was sure that he had a mental score-card for every time he brought her to orgasm. He was an accomplished lover and a patient teacher. It would only be a matter of a few years before Barbara discovered that in this bedroom sport, there were home games, but there were a lot of away games too. Remembering those betrayals was still so painful that the interruption of her daydreaming was a good thing. It meant there was no time to revisit the heartbreak of being unable to conceive a child, of Ellis's refusal to adopt, and of course, of the many affairs she knew he'd had since she was elected to the bench.

She was aware that people in the courthouse gossiped about their marriage, but maybe they'd never been as deeply, absurdly in love as she was with Ellis. And he knew how to play her perfectly. There was always the argument, followed by the apology, and then the unbelievable sex that left her exhausted but trembling for more as morning came. It was beyond ratio-nality, especially for a sophisticated, educated woman. And it was embarrassing. She knew a fair amount about battered women, had read reports describing their apparent willing-ness to tolerate repeated episodes of abuse and then later excuse the abuser's violence and return for more. She was beginning to understand this seemingly bizarre behavior, and that alone was a sign that she needed help from a professional.

The knock on the door was longer and louder. It was time for her to leave and return to Tallahassee to finish her special assignment. She only hoped there would be no more excitement here at the court. As long as she could stay away, she didn't need to look at her bedside clock when she heard Ellis come in just before dawn.

|12|

AMY COHEN NEVER expected a minor fender bender to change her life—let alone end it. It was late March, and Detroit streets were slippery, as usual, and crowded. She leaned forward in her small yellow VW to see through the space at the bottom of the windshield. "Shit!" she yelled to no one. "I can't see a fucking thing in front of me!" That came just before the unmistakable sensation of contact with the rear bumper ahead of her.

Amy would later consider the collision a blessing in disguise. Divorced twice already at the age of thirty, alienated from her parents, who never stopped talking about her dead brother, and unable to find work that paid anything but pennies, she was desperate for a source of support—both financial and emotional. When a tall, attractive young man stepped out of the Honda that now sported a large rear fender dent, she was prepared for the worst. She expected him to stagger around, grabbing at his neck and shoulders while yelling "Whiplash!" at the small line of cars trapped by their minor collision. To her great surprise and considerable relief, he came toward her with a goofy smile on his face and extended his hand. "Helluva way to pick guys up, but whatever. It's your America."

Amy knew otherwise, but she kept her flaws, her fears, and a history of risk-taking and bad judgment to herself. Josiah did the same. They both learned much later and much too late that what you see is not always what you get. But only he would live to tell the tale.

Josiah lived in a part of Detroit that Amy had never seen, and if she had, she would have locked her doors at the first intersection. They desperately wanted to live together, but Amy's room at a residential hotel, where she was the youngest person by decades, wouldn't do, and she wasn't about to cave and beg her rich parents for a handout. When Josiah suggested a move to Florida, Amy jumped around his lumpy mattress like a kid who was going to Disney World. In fact, Orlando was their first stop in Florida. They had fantasized about landing jobs at one of the theme parks. Their first encounter with the reality of the Sunshine State was at the Universal employment office. "You and ten thousand other people! These aren't jobs, my friends—these are career moves, and unless you're prepared to commit to us, we're definitely not prepared to do anything for you." The elderly man with rimless glasses had barely looked at them as he slid a folder across the counter. "Can't blame you, though. Could be the best place to work in the world. Whoops! I meant to say universe."

They worked their way south on I-95, thinking that Miami could make room for them, despite their lack of marketable skills. Amy had never had a job more serious than the stockroom at the mall, and Josiah was equally unskilled. An ad for a dental assistant in the *Miami Herald* caught Amy's eye, and no sooner had she been hired, entirely based on the fact that she was decent looking and spoke English, than Josiah found work at a gated community, hauling branches and dead landscaping for a gardening group. They laughed at the absurdity of their native tongue becoming their greatest asset. That and their citizenship. What a hoot!

Their relationship was intense, made all the more so by the recreational drugs they both enjoyed and their mutual, outspoken disdain for the church, the government, and whatever else didn't seem to fit their lifestyle. Josiah's family was discussed only once, and that was for the purpose of impressing on Amy that they were a bunch of losers, were not worth the time of day, and would be better off in the hereafter. Amy was equally reticent about her parents, but she was eager to tell Josiah about her dead brother, Michael. She recounted their competitions as children, contests about everything from who could hold their breath for the longest time to who could steal from the small change her father always deposited on his dresser top and get away with it. Describing their escapades took her to another place, and it was a place with no room for Josiah. Her reminiscences aroused feelings of rejection and loneliness in him. And he, in turn, looked to ways to punish her for, as he put it, making him feel "like a piece of shit."

The resolution of these disturbances usually involved getting high. The higher they were, the better the sex that followed. But the arguments were becoming more violent and more predictable, from rants about her privileged childhood (and his impoverished one) to his obsession with Nazi folklore and her paranoia about the swastika flags and army decorations that hung around the house.

They were both unhappy. They both felt trapped. And Amy, for the first time in her life, yearned for the safety she had left behind in Bloomfield Hills. When she allowed herself to think about her parents, she realized how deeply shocked and dismayed they would be by her lifestyle and the violence in her home.

She would not live long enough to see their shock or the murderous rage on her father's face, her father who blamed God and Josiah in exactly that order. No one would see it, at least not in time to do anything about it.

|13|

CASEY STARED INTO the mirror above her bathroom sink as though the face looking back at her could give her some answers. She was thrilled to be in a relationship with Luke Anderson. He was ten years her senior, but the age difference didn't seem to matter to either of them. And she had no misgivings that she was suffering from some kind of father-figure attraction. But she was uncomfortable with the fact that he had been married and divorced. She was frequently on the verge of asking questions about his ex-wife, but she sensed that she was in unsafe territory, and she admired the fact that Luke never spoke negatively about his former life.

But with all Luke's maturity and experience, he could no more help her answer the questions about what she really wanted in life than the mirror could. Knowing that she had a reasonably good brain, a good sense of humor, and an attraction to excitement was a state of being, but it was hardly what you'd call a plan. She was envious of women like Janet Kanterman and Barbara Clarke, women who had all of what she liked about herself plus all the qualities she worried that she lacked. She had strong views on politics, values, and conduct, just as Janet and Barbara seemed to have, but they seemed more grounded, more certain of who they were and where they were headed.

It was ironic that her romance with Luke intensified her confusion about whether she wanted the easier path of marriage and kids—a path many of her friends had already chosen—or a career that might remove that option, at best, or leave her caught between the two worlds for most of her adult life.

She put her toothbrush onto its charging stand and pulled the towel tight around her. She now knew one thing for certain about herself: she liked sex, and she liked it strong, fast, and, well, sexy. Most of all she liked it with Luke. She opened the door to her small but neatly appointed bedroom, hoping that her morning routine might have awakened him. No such luck. He lay facing her with the sheet pulled up to his chin and one leg falling over the side of the bed.

Too bad, she thought. *I'll have to do without this morning.* As she opened the door into the hallway, she vaguely spotted a glimpse of hair before she was caught from behind and pulled down to the floor. "Jesus H. Christ," she screamed, "are you completely nuts?"

He gently but firmly lifted her off the floor and then unceremoniously dumped her on the bed. As she bounced up, he dove down. "Oh, my god. Oh, god," she moaned as first his fingers and then his tongue made their way into her. "You're going to drown down there!" she yelled.

If he said anything, she never heard it. Whatever sensory

input her ears were capable of was nothing compared to the cornucopia of nerve endings she had discovered in the rest of her body. Her capacity for pleasure had grown so rapidly that it was often Casey who reached climax before Luke. She discovered another well-kept secret when that happened. Unlike the male of the species, her body was the gift that kept on giving, as one after another orgasm rippled through her.

She knew she couldn't be late this morning, not for the first day of jury selection. So when they finally pulled apart, sweaty and smelling strongly of sex, she reached for the spray cologne, doused herself, dressed, and walked out the door looking like she knew exactly who she was and just what she wanted.

|14|

ALTHOUGH THE PROSECUTION and defense attorneys had been instructed by the court to produce a jury questionnaire in a very short time, neither side had any real difficulty creating their list of questions. Lawyers who charge clients for the time spent preparing motions, briefs, or other court documents rarely share the simple truth that most of these documents are on their computers already and merely require a name, date, and courtroom change on the cover page. If a newer lawyer doesn't have the right software, the Internet will provide a treasure trove of well-written filings to download in minutes. A jury questionnaire can be found at a dozen sites and usually needs little more creative energy than narrowing the focus of the document to fit the facts of the trial.

The voir dire, or examination of prospective jurors, that uses the answers to written questions as the starting point is standard in many respects and beyond the obvious questions, the real intent of the exercise is to weed out the nutcases, identify people with an axe to grind, and get the desired balance of gender, race, and age that will be most advantageous for your side. That balance depends on a number of factors, including the nature of the case, the race and gender of the accused and of the victim, and the sympathies aroused by the case. The sorting process also includes questioning the fitness of people in certain professions, such as members of the clergy who might be overly sympathetic to defendants, or retired cops who had seen it all before. Then there are the stealth jurors. No one can properly prepare for the prospective juror who appears to be God's gift to the legal system. These are often *Law and Order* junkies, and they know how to game the system and ensure that they snag a seat on the jury.

Both sides are also keenly aware that many courts, especially the federal bench, have dramatically limited the involvement of attorneys in the jury selection process. Some judges have openly expressed their annoyance at lawyers who attempt to influence the prospective jurors before the trial has begun. Attorneys, on the other hand, resent the interference in what they regard as an important opportunity to make a good impression on jurors and to test their theories about the case.

The "Dogicide" trial presented some special challenges. Although there had been several murder cases involving pit bulls, this was the first such case in Florida and the first where a claim of incompetence had been raised by the defense. Although at least two psychological evaluations of the defendant had been conducted, the defense theory relied on a sort of *non compos mentes,* Latin for "out of your mind." That made this a case of first impression, relying on law that was novel and without clear precedent. Charlie Graham's assistants and law clerks had spent days researching the history of homicides involving animals of all kinds in a variety of settings. The use of poisonous insects and snakes to rid oneself of an unwanted spouse or lover occurred with some frequency in fiction and was a theory, although unproven, in some early cases of assault, but there was no case where the state alleged an intentional murder using a dog as a weapon and the defendant claimed to be present in physical form only, having no memory of the incident at all. Finally, it raised a long list of other potential problems, not the least of which was the affection that many of the prospective jurors might have for animals in general, and for dogs in particular.

Josiah Diemert's defense team wanted to keep all pet owners off the jury, and although they employed a small battalion of summer associates to research ways to accomplish this, it was obvious that such a request to exclude this particular subset of the population was unlikely to succeed. The state, of course, wanted nothing more than to keep those same people on the jury.

Charlie Graham was determined that this case would go in clean, meaning that no bias, prejudice, or misconduct on the state's part could poison the outcome. A guilty verdict—, or, for that matter, a guilty plea to the lesser crime of manslaughter—, would give his career a major boost. The flip side of that was mega-failure, which in this case meant either a not- guilty verdict or a mistrial. It was the specter of the latter that had kept Charlie out of bed most of last night.

Yesterday afternoon, a woman had appeared at the intake desk situated just inside the glass door to the State Attorney's office. She insisted on speaking to Charlie Graham about the murder trial. This last-minute appearance by someone claiming to have crucial evidence was not the least bit unusual. It actually happened frequently, especially with high-profile cases. Lead prosecutors like Charlie Graham almost never responded to these visits or phone calls, and this case was no exception. Instead of going directly to Charlie's office, the woman, who introduced herself as Phyllis Cohen Hersch, was led to a small conference room by a young intern whose job was to "take some notes and get rid of her."

It took less than two minutes for the young man to race-walk to his boss's office and drag him into the conference room. Phyllis Hersch was a soft-spoken woman in her mid-fifties. She spoke haltingly of her relationship with her now-deceased great-niece and her estrangement from her cousin, Harold Cohen, and his wife, Miriam. She was grieving for them all, she said, because she had agreed nearly five years earlier to assume custody of Amy's newborn child, a child who knew nothing of her birth mother and whose grand-parents, Harold and Miriam, probably knew nothing of her.

According to Mrs. Hersch, Amy came to her for help when she discovered that she was pregnant, fearing that her parents would reject this baby and leave her without any way to live and support the two of them. Phyllis agreed to take care of the baby until Amy got on her feet or found the courage to tell her parents. Although she and Amy had been in touch for a few years, Amy had claimed that she was too broke to visit her child and too scared of her father's temper to confront him with this shocking news. "Was I wrong? Should I have called Harold and Miriam?" She looked plead-ingly at Charlie and the young intern, who had no answers, only questions.

Charlie's mind was racing. Did the defense team know? Was this evidence they had to disclose? Was it evidence, in fact, of anything more than unprotected sex by the victim?

Did it make Amy Cohen less of a victim? Did it make Josiah Diemert less of a killer? Given the power of this surprise information, no one in the State Attorney's office knew the answer, and no one really wanted to ask.

|15|

JUDGE KANTERMAN'S COURTROOM was packed. The jury office had sent fifty prospective jurors upstairs, and they had filled every available seat, including those in the jury box. They spilled into the aisles and into the clerks' box as well. There was understandably a great deal of noise, and Casey resorted to the judge's gavel to try for some order.

"Excuse me, excuse me!" she shouted as she pounded the gavel. "I need everyone's attention." She was relieved to see that most of the crowd had stopped talking and there were a few volunteer "shushers" who had come to her aid.

"As you were told downstairs, you are here to be questioned for a possible seat on the jury that will hear this case. Because the charges in this case involve a possible life sentence, we will seat twelve jurors instead of the usual six. Each of you has received a written questionnaire which you must complete before court opens. If you need help, please let one of the staff know, and we will assist you. Please listen carefully, as this is most important. Judge Kanterman will be taking the bench in just a moment to welcome you and to swear you in as prospective jurors. From that moment on, you are a part of this trial, and whether you are selected to serve or not, you may not discuss this case or anything you have heard or seen related to it until the case has concluded. Do you all understand?" Casey heard the chorus of "Yes," "All right," and "Got it," but she knew that there were those in the crowd who couldn't wait to get on the line to Aunt Tilley and talk about the trial. "Oh, well, we do our best," she muttered to herself as she mounted the stairs to the judge's bench to open court. "Hear ye, hear ye . . ."

Harold Cohen was pressed against the far back wall. He was desperate for a look at this judge who everyone claimed was such a flaming liberal that she would more than likely find a reason to acquit his daughter's killer. He wasn't about to let that happen. Not even if it meant he might spend the rest of his life in jail for committing murder himself.

The judge climbed the steps and took her seat above the packed courtroom, above the press, the witness chair, and the array of deputy sheriffs. She opened a book on her desk and began a lengthy recitation of the obligations of service on a jury, especially in a murder trial. She spoke in a monotone, and a number of the prospective jurors had closed their eyes or were surreptitiously reading a folded newspaper or a paperback. Luke Anderson was standing near the back door of the courtroom with Ben, Judge Clarke's bailiff, and both men were surprised by the judge's lack of energy and enthusiasm. This was not the Janet Kanterman they knew. Luke turned to Ben and whispered, "Hey, what gives with the judge? She's usually a cross between an evangelist and Darth Vader when she instructs the new recruits to the jury pool."

Ben turned his face slightly but kept his eyes forward. "Can't really tell. I know that she's been complaining about her stomach to Casey, but she's up there doing her thing."

Casey called out, "All rise," to the room, which had become uncomfortably warm. When the cable news guys raised their right hands to be sworn, the judge provided the only light moment of the day by telling them to sit down, since the electronic media already thought that they were judge and jury and needed no further encouragement. Once the prospective jurors had been sworn, the judge left the bench, and Casey called a recess until after lunch to allow jurors to fill out the questionnaire agreed to by both sides.

The room began to empty, as the media had no interest in the jurors, and just about everyone else had gone to attend to other business. Ben waved good-bye to Casey, who was assisting a nearly deaf juror who had missed the better part of the instructions and had no idea what she had just sworn to do for her country. As Ben left Judge Kanterman's courtroom to return to his own desk across the hall, a hand fell firmly on his shoulder. Startled, he spun around and found a face that he never would have expected to see again in this courthouse.

"What the fuck are you doing here? Have you lost your mind—or rather, what's left of it?"

"Mind your manners, son. You may have the power, but I've got the pills! So don't you do your uppity crap with me." Jack McGinty turned and headed toward the bank of elevators. Before he reached the first door, Ben was beside him. Stains had already formed under Ben's shirtsleeves, and a powerful stink of fear was rising like heat from the gutter on an August day.

"Jack, I'm sorry. Please. I'm under a lot of pressure here, man. I'm really sorry." McGinty tossed a Safeway shopping bag over his shoulder; Ben caught it in mid-air and, without looking back, sprinted across the small lobby and through the double glass doors and collapsed in his desk chair. Ben Toledo was a trapped man. He knew it. Worse than that, some really badass people knew it too.

|16|

JANET OPENED THE glove compartment while her eyes remained fixed on the road. The Kleenex pack and her Elton John and Sarah Brightman CDs came spilling out to the floor beneath the passenger seat. She didn't give up and kept groping until the she heard the rattle. *Hallelujah,* she thought as the Pepcid AC Maximum Strength slid out of its corner and into her hand. As she got purchase on the top by holding it against the wheel with her elbow while unscrewing it with the other hand, she remembered how indifferent her husband, Stuart, had been to all the warning signs of a cataclysmic cardiac arrest. The potbelly, the breathlessness, the chest pain when he got too excited watching a Miami Dolphins fourth-quarter Hail Mary pass. She had tried all the known motivators—the begging, the threats, the cognitive stuff, the "think about me and the children." Nothing had worked, and sometimes late at night when she thought about him, when her hands slipped beneath the sheet and blanket to the waiting emptiness and need, she wondered if his resistance to taking care of himself was a kind of death wish. After all, not every legal assistance lawyer (*i.e.,* low paid, overworked) ends up married to a superstar who is appointed to and then elected to retain a seat on the circuit trial court.

The car behind her blasted away as she sat too long at the light, downing her antacid pills and daydreaming. As she pulled away, Janet replayed her conversation with Judge Marks earlier that morning.

"I don't envy you. None of us on this bench is used to such a complicated case." While Janet was surprised to hear these empathetic remarks, she was more than a little taken aback when Marks continued by commenting on rumors that the stress was affecting her health. She despised the courthouse gossip that was a constant reminder that they were elected, not appointed, to their high office. Every judge was aware that there were lawyers or lower court judges waiting in the wings for their opportunity to secure a place in the hearts of the voters. Bad publicity, whether it came as rumors of infidelity, theft in office, laziness, or health problems, could create that opening. Walking away, Janet had glanced back over her shoulder, immediately regretting her failure to deny the rumors about her health. She nevertheless was a little unnerved that the courthouse gossip was more accurate than not. She felt rotten. She had terrible pain in her midsection, especially around mid-morning and late afternoon. She suspected it was the coffee that she loved so much, but that made no sense, since she had been a bean addict for as long as she could remember with no bad effects. In any event, she promised herself that as soon as possible, and certainly once this god-awful trial ended, she would call her physician to schedule an appointment.

In the meantime she smiled, remembering her son's suggestion to her in a recent e-mail. "It's not healthy to be alone, Mom, and we all think you should consider going on the Internet to see if there are some eligible men down there." She knew they meant well, but she had no interest in another man at this point in her life. The thought of sex with anyone but Stuart terrified and repulsed her. Almost sixty-five, she was content to finish her next term on the bench and spend her time reading and listening to music. But she had said none of that to her firstborn son. She simply thanked him for his interest and assured him that she was in perfect health.

When the now-familiar clutch of pain tore at her stomach, she wished that she had told him the truth. But then again, this was just stress speaking to her through her body. She'd get past this and get a checkup and a much-needed rest.

She assumed it could wait until then.

|17|

THE JURY OFFICE at the Justice Complex is a decorator's nightmare. Narrow hallways lead to small rooms and painted walls with nothing on them but the scrapings from the cheap metal chairs that are scattered around the equally unattractive tables. There is no comfortable seating unless you consider the sizeable movie theater a place to lounge or nap while you await the call from one of the courtrooms above the third floor. The entrance to the jury area is equally unattractive. It is dominated by a high, flat, unadorned metal desk behind which are the clerks who mail Notices to Appear.

Jury service in Palm Beach County is expected of everyone who has a driver's license, since it is through the random selection of licenses that prospective jurors are drawn. There is a long list of excuses, however, including age, infirmity, and job requirements, that provide an escape route. Fortunately, most people see their one-day or one-trial commitment as a necessary evil. They make the best of it.

The local press in Palm Beach had carried extensive coverage of the bombing incident and the people signing in for jury duty were visibly nervous. There was ongoing chatter about the wisdom of holding court in these circumstances, let alone asking innocent citizens to be sitting ducks. But one young, attractive, and scantily dressed member of the jury pool was completely disinterested in the bombing—or, for that matter, anything having to do with the judicial system. What mattered to her and what had really pissed her off was the warning sign that no cell phones or beepers were permitted in the courtrooms or the jury office.

What a joke, she thought. *As if we're going to disappear off the face of the earth for this crap!* Brittany was registered as juror number 33, a number she found extremely boring, but then she was easily bored, a fact that her parents attributed to her superior intelligence and that her teachers saw as the result of too much television. Despite a flurry of phone calls to her influential clients at the tanning salon where she worked, she had been unable to avoid appearing for her stint as a good citizen.

She was surprised to see young people milling around the room or waiting in line for a shot at one of the plug-ins for their computers. She had assumed that the place would be populated by the geriatric set, too old to have a real job and too young for the nursing home. She was especially gratified by the looks she got from some of the men, since she had not taken the time this morning to perform her usual extended makeup and hair routine. Still, the long, silky, brown ponytail that swung in arcs across her back seemed to have the usual hypnotic affect on the male population in the room. Her Irish skin had none of the ruddiness associated with that gene, owing largely to long hours with the tanning beds that she managed for the beauty salon.

Brittany possessed a hard-edged version of what people called "street smarts," and she had already sized up the situation at the courthouse. She figured that if she got lucky, she would be dumped from service for God-knows-what reason, and she could go back to the tanning salon as if nothing had ever happened. If she was actually picked for a jury, she'd make sure that she got out in time to put in her hours at the salon—either selling time on the beds or using them herself. Meanwhile, she was chatting up a not-so-bad-looking dude seated at a table across from her. She rolled her eyes toward the high, stained ceiling. "I hear we may be called for this murder case. It's not as if I knew this girl. Hello-o-o? How do you let a dog make dinner out of you, for Christ's sake?" The dude never got a chance to answer. The loudspeaker was blaring with the latest instructions for the trapped citizens.

The prospective jurors were being called up to Kanterman's courtroom in groups of twenty-five, so if a jury wasn't seated out of the first group, Brittany knew she was headed upstairs. Since they had been told that this trial needed not only the usual twelve jurors, but six alternates as well, she was pretty sure she'd get her chance to check out the scene.

Brittany had no sooner returned to her *InStyle Magazine* than the fat lady sang out the news that a fresh batch of jury meat was needed for Judge Kanterman's trial and that jurors 26 to 50 should line up in the order of their numbers.

Brittany scooped up her magazines, her oversized gold and silver lamé purse, and the remains of her Wendy's burger. Her cell phone was on silent, so unless they had to go through metal detectors again, she could keep her lifeline open. She was so adept at texting that it was almost impossible to detect her moving fingers.

When they arrived at the courtroom, it was pretty

obvious that a lot of their comrades had escaped. The front row had only nine people, which meant that sixteen people had left for one reason or another. *Lucky ducks,* she thought as they were lined up like schoolchildren on their way to recess.

Once they were seated numerically, Charlie Graham introduced himself and his team and explained that they and the defense attorneys were going to be asking them questions, mostly based on their answers to the questionnaires. When everyone was finished, the attorneys could ask the judge to excuse some jurors who couldn't serve because of disabilities, work, or home problems. Rarely, a juror would be excused because one or both lawyers convinced the judge that the juror was too prejudiced or knew too much about the case. Finally, each side got a chance to remove some jurors without giving any reason at all. If they still didn't have the required number of people, a new batch of recruits from the jury room would be brought upstairs.

Brittany didn't hear a lot of Charlie Graham's explanation, because she couldn't take her eyes off the man seated across the courtroom at a long table. He didn't look much like a lawyer, but then she didn't know many lawyers from the tanning salon where she worked. The guy Brittany was staring at was wearing a suit and tie, very businesslike, but something about him was absolutely terrifying her. He sat like a stiff, a dead guy, looking down at the table the entire time. Just then the guy swung around in his chair as though he could feel her eyes on him. "Holy shit! This guy is totally wasted!" Brittany dropped her eyes fast and didn't look at the guy again until she was told to move up to the front row for questioning. It was when Lloyd Schwartzman made the defense team introductions that Brittany found out who the guy was and decided then and there that whatever they said he'd done, he'd done.

When the lawyers began to question what she had come

to think of as her "batch," Brittany was paying a lot more attention, especially when they began asking about dogs; who had them, how they felt about animals, whether anyone had been bitten or attacked by a dog, and on and on. "Holy Mother of God," she muttered under her breath, "did this joker murder his dog, too?"

"Ma'am," Graham began, "I gather from your questionnaire that you have never served on a jury before. Is that correct?"

"No," said Brittany. Everyone's head seemed to jerk up at once. "I mean, like, no, I haven't been on a jury before, so I guess I mean yes." Brittany heard the suppressed laughter and felt her cheeks burning.

"That's all right, young lady. Please don't be nervous. I'd say we weren't going to bite you, but in this case that wouldn't be so funny."

"Objection!" Lloyd Schwartzman was on his feet.

Judge Kanterman looked up from her notes and stared at Schwartzman. "Counselor?" she inquired hesitantly. It was obvious to everyone in the courtroom that the judge had not been paying attention.

Before the court could ask the basis for the objection, Charlie Graham turned toward the bench and said, "I apologize, Your Honor. I made a stupid joke, and I withdraw it, and hope it will be stricken."

"Done," said the judge and resumed reading. Graham breathed a sigh of relief. If Lloyd had wanted to, he could have insisted that the remark had poisoned the minds of all the prospective jurors currently in the room and demanded that they begin the whole process anew. As Graham looked over at the defense table, he thought, not for the first time, that Lloyd despised his client. *Well, I always knew he had some taste,* thought Graham as he turned back to continue his questioning of the very attractive Ms. Brittany McGinty.

|18|

OPENING STATEMENTS ARE a critical part of any trial, especially for the prosecution. They set the stage, prepare the jury for the evidence that the state plans to introduce, and lay down the building blocks for the case.

The day following jury selection in *State of Florida vs. Josiah Diemert,* the courtroom was full as Charlie Graham stood and faced the jury to make his Opening Statement. But as good as he was that morning, nothing could fully describe the horrific events of July 26. That was true, in part, because much of what had happened was known to only two people, and one of them was dead. What was known came from a variety of sources, including neighbors, co-workers, and to a great extent, long interrogations of the defendant.

Amy and Josiah had been living together for over a year. For Christmas, Josiah had brought home a puppy, a pit bull known as a brindle. Amy wanted to name the dog Joe, short for Josiah. Josiah would have none of it.

"This doggie is going to be big, baby, and I want a big name. In fact, I'm gonna call him Butch."

Amy thought naming a dog after a haircut was stupid, but she had learned better than to argue with Josiah. He could be a laid-back, easy kind of guy one minute and a raging maniac the next. There wasn't any clear pattern to his behavior, and he was so apologetic after he hit her or stormed out of the house, often disappearing for hours, that she felt sorry for him. When he brought up the idea of getting a dog, she quickly agreed. Maybe the distraction of a puppy would calm things down.

Throughout that spring, the dog was the focus of their attention and their affection. Butch actually seemed to like her company better, a fact that she downplayed in front of Josiah. By early May, Butch indeed became a large dog, and having successfully housebroken him, Josiah was now training him to "jump" a small bush in their yard on command. One of the neighbors complained to her that Josiah yelling "Attack!" and "Release!" at all hours was scaring her kids. It was spooking Amy too, but she and Josiah were bickering all the time now, and she was beginning to think she'd made another huge mistake. He wanted Amy to call her father and get some money. "What the fuck! Your old man's loaded, and you're his only kid."

Amy had never been a hard-core druggie. She was too timid to do crack or heroin. Josiah, on the other hand, would do anything that crossed his path, as long as he wasn't at work and it wouldn't cost him much. She stuck to her long-standing drugs of choice: the opiods, weed, and alcohol of any kind. If she hadn't lost her job, it might have worked for a little while longer. Getting sacked was her secret, just one of many she kept from Josiah. She wasn't really sure why she also had never told him about her daughter. She loved Josiah, at least as much as she had ever loved anyone except her brother, but she had an uneasy feeling about him. He talked too much and too often about her father's money and he kept pressing her to call her parents and say they were a happily married couple—when, in fact, they were neither married nor happy.

Sometime in late June, Amy had been caught lifting sample painkillers from the dentist's desk drawer. Her tearful entreaties persuaded him to not call the cops, but of course he fired her on the spot. Now, nearly a month and dozens of dead-end job applications later, she was tired of her secrets and so low on cash that even a small half-pint of cheap vodka was not in the picture. Amy decided that she no longer had a choice. Her hands were shaking uncontrollably, but she hit the call button and waited to hear the ring.

Miriam Cohen picked up the phone with her trademark hello, a singsong greeting that sounded like an aria. Amy froze. Her mother's second greeting was more tentative than the first, and this time Amy whispered, "It's me, Mom." She could hear her mother's sharp intake of breath, could almost feel the heave of her chest.

"Amy," she sobbed. "Oh, my god, Amy, where are you? Are you all right? Oh, my god. Oh, my god." Her mother's voice trailed off, and now Amy was holding the cell phone away from her ear, as far away as she could, until she hit the red button to end the call.

When Amy got home earlier than usual, she expected questions about the time and her job, but Josiah was actually happy to see her, a change from his usual irritable response to her presence.

"Wassup, babe?" he slurred as he rolled on his side. *Shit,* he thought, *I'm so fucking mellow, I might be able to get it up.*

As if she'd read his thoughts, Amy crossed over to the

couch, leaned her face down to his, and blew hot air at him. "Wassup is your stupid fucking free ride. You can go grab that stinking animal of yours and get out of here. The pony ride is over, asshole."

She'd often heard the expression "in a heartbeat," but that's how fast the blow came. What was really surprising was the time lapse before she felt the pain. But it came like a locomotive running through her mouth straight to the back of her head. As her head snapped back, she lost her balance and began to flop like a circus clown mimicking a drunk. When she finally stumbled onto the coffee table and slid to the floor, the second blow, this one to her belly, caused such searing pain and nausea that it worked in her favor—not what Josiah was looking for. She knew this pattern, knew the beats and the rhythm of his rage. It didn't always begin this way; usually it was a slap on the arm or a yank at her hair. But it always escalated from wherever it started, and it never let up until he became so sweaty, breathless, and hysterical that he scared himself into retreat or she passed out or pretended to pass out. This time she was having none of it. Not this time.

Amy rolled on her side, moaning and gagging for effect, knowing he'd pause to relish her pain. Sure enough, the room became still except for her histrionics and his heavy breathing. And then she made the break. She rolled farther away, still moaning in agony, then abruptly stood and raced out the door before Josiah had processed what he was seeing plainly.

She didn't call for help. She didn't go to a neighbor. She simply ran, knowing that the last thing she wanted was the police—or, for that matter, anyone—messing in their business. After all, the amount of drugs and drug paraphernalia lying around that house would put them both away for years—if they were lucky.

She needn't have worried about any good Samaritans

reaching out to help. Most of the neighborhood knew about the Diemerts and wanted to steer clear of them and their dog. Even if they hadn't heard the screaming and the fights, the sight of this woman covered in blood and crying hysterically was enough to cause anyone to run the other way.

Amy cursed herself for panicking and leaving without her car keys or cell phone. She reached into the pocket of her once-white (now bloodstained) nurse's pants and found what she prayed would be there—the change from the hot dog vendor outside the Walgreens store where she killed time pretending to be at work. "Please let it be enough," she prayed. Her hands were shaking so badly that the coins wrapped inside the paper money came spilling out and bounced musically across the pavement. As Amy scrambled to retrieve the nickels and dimes, she muttered a running accounting. "If I can just get into a movie, I can fall asleep and pray that he goes out with his buddies and drinks himself into a stupor."

She had always loved going to the movies. Her brother, Michael, had loved it too, and after he was killed, she felt as though she was cheating him if she did "their" Saturday afternoon triple feature without him. They were ardent Trekkies and *Star Wars* fans and never missed a sci-fi film, an obsession totally lost on their parents, who thought *Invasion of the Body Snatchers* was as futuristic as movies could get.

Right now, though, Amy would settle for Bugs Bunny. As she approached the box office, she checked herself in the window of Alvie's Delicatessen and was relieved to find that her face, although swollen, was not bloody and her eye had not yet blackened.

The young man behind the window of the box office looked like a before picture for an acne treatment. Amy felt immediate pity for him. She could only imagine how self-conscious he was, and she wished she could tell him how much worse life could get than some unruly pimples. Amy saw that she was short a dollar for a ticket, and she was sure the boy would not buy the idea that she was a senior citizen. She looked down at the blood on her nurse's pants and, sighing audibly, said, "I just got off work. Emergency nurse, ya know? Couldn't save the poor guy, and I need a break before I go back for more gore. Would you mind helping an angel of mercy and let me in for half price? I promise I won't stay for the whole movie. I just need a break, man."

Amy stepped back so he could get a good look at the blood. He didn't say a word, just turned to look over his shoulder and pressed the button to eject a ticket. Amy grabbed it and, without another word, walked quickly into the theater. She never even saw the name of the movie. She entered the darkened theater and was asleep in less than a minute. It was almost four hours later when she felt a hand shaking her roughly.

"Hey, lady, wake up, will ya? This ain't no hotel. Get the fuck outta here before I call the cops."

Amy sputtered as she sat up. An older man was standing over her. The lights were on in the theater, and it was just the two of them.

"Jesus, what happened to you?"

Amy was pretty sure her injuries had become a great deal more obvious, and she made an effort to pull herself out of the seat. "Sorry," she muttered, "I just needed a place to pull myself together."

The man looked her over carefully. "Listen, honey. I got a place upstairs where I can fix you up a little. We can have a drink, and you can relax there for a while. Whaddaya say?"

She knew better than to say yes. Every still-functioning part of her brain was on red alert. But that alarm system our parents hardwire into us was ignored by Amy, as it had been dismissed so many times before in her life. This time, however, the fates were playing for keeps.

19

JOSIAH NODDED OFF through most of Graham's Opening Statement, a fact not entirely lost on the jurors. His nap was ended abruptly by an elbow in his ribs. He looked over to see his lawyer glowering at him. "Sit up, for chrissakes, and open your eyes. I don't give a shit what your daydreams are about, but you're damn well not going to nod me out of a defense." Schwartzman stood and requested a recess for lunch so that he could confer with his client and co-counsel. In the jury box, Brittany was feverishly texting and failed to hear the call for a recess—until she received a similar elbow shot from her neighbor.

As the courtroom cleared, Casey was surprised to see Luke move swiftly toward the bench. "I need to speak with the judge, and you should be there as well. Judge Marks is on his way down to join us." Casey knew better than to ask questions when Luke was in his law enforcement mode. She doubted that anyone knew about their relationship, but she wasn't about to risk exposure, at least not at this point, before she had any idea where things were going—and, for that matter, where she wanted them to go.

Judge Marks, accompanied by his bailiff, went directly into Kanterman's chambers, followed by Luke, who motioned to Casey to follow. No one sat down. "I've got some disturbing news that Judge Marks is already aware of. Apparently an article appeared in the *Miami Herald* about the trial. It was mostly the usual report of jury selection and witnesses. That would have been just fine, had it stopped there, but the reporter went on to describe specific plans to euthanize the dog as soon as the case began. The article was picked up on the Internet, and what was a local concern among so-called dog lovers has now gone national—and in a very nasty way."

Judge Kanterman was the first to sit down. "I've been concerned about a YouTube backlash since our little bombing incident several days ago."

"Little bombing incident, my glorious ass!" Judge Marks exploded. "We're under siege here, and—no animal puns intended—we're sitting ducks for these lunatics."

Luke raised his hand like a traffic cop and turned toward Marks. "Look, Judge, there's no sense going and getting yourself and everyone else into an uproar about this. We need to make some plans for better security and for moving this case along as quickly as possible. That's why we're meeting, and I need some cooperation."

Marks turned toward Luke. "I don't like your tone of voice, mister, but we'll address that at another time. Since Judge Spellman has asked me to deal with the safety issue, I'm prepared to work on a plan with your department and present it to the court for approval soon as humanly possible.

You and I can meet separately on that. As for moving the case along, well . . ." Marks's glance was a glare, openly challenging Judge Kanterman to respond.

Janet looked intently at her shoes. It was a temper-control trick she had learned long ago as a young lawyer when opposing counsel would begin to verbally browbeat the "lady lawyer" at a deposition or hearing. She'd pretend she had X-ray vision and could count her toes. This seemed like as good a time as any to use it. When she found ten of them present and accounted for, she looked up at the group gathered around her desk. "There is no way to *speed up* a first-degree murder case, other than to hold night court, and I have no intention of doing that. Jury selection is complete, and the jury is sworn, so the case will go forward, absent some bizarre occurrence that would require a mistrial. I don't expect that to happen, and frankly, I do expect that our enhanced security will eliminate the necessity to rush through this trial or alter it in any substantial way."

She was as wrong as wrong could be.

20

THERE WAS NO reason for Janet to remain at the courthouse late on the night in question. Court had adjourned
for the day, the half-sheets had been signed and delivered
to Casey for filing the next morning, and there were no
pending motions that needed her immediate attention. No,
it was more a lingering unease about a long list of things
that persuaded her to remain behind her desk well after the
background noise of the courthouse had diminished and
eventually disappeared.

The elderly black woman who usually cleaned had yet
to appear and request permission to vacuum (a largely
futile endeavor, given the tracked-in dirt that formed a
patina on the rugged carpet that ran without interruption

through the hallways and the judges' chambers) and her late arrival gave Janet the few quiet moments she felt she needed to sort some things out.

She had been particularly disturbed by her encounter with Ben earlier in the day. She was fond of the gangly bailiff and had been concerned by his distant and withdrawn behavior over the last several days. She had chided him for "poisoning" the coffee that he provided to her and Casey nearly every morning. Not only did Ben not laugh at the joke (all of the staff on the floor knew she was suffering from recurrent bouts of digestive distress), but he also turned a deep, embarrassed red. Added to his apparent discomfort was his attitude when Janet asked yet again for the file and journal regarding the disposition of the vehicular homicide case.

"For chrissakes," Ben almost shouted, "what is the big deal about that case? I'll have to dig through files and computer notes to satisfy your curiosity about something that's not even on your docket!"

It was not impossible to alter records at court, not even those that have been scanned or uploaded to the computer system. In the old days, making a minor change to the length of probation or the size of a fine was a piece of cake. The hard drive of the system now in place was intended to prevent such abuses. Its reputation as foolproof had evidently aroused the competitive nature of some court personnel, however, because every now and then someone turned up in a jail in Alabama when they were supposed to be in downtown West Palm. Judges were naturally anxious when they couldn't reconcile their recollections or files with the computer screen.

"I beg your pardon," Janet calmly replied, "the case is technically on my docket because Judge Clarke is away from the court. I'm not asking anymore. I am ordering you to get those documents to me, or I'll have to discuss the matter with Judge Clarke." Janet had watched Ben as he stormed across to the elevator, and she resolved to find out what was bothering him. She promised herself to ask Casey in the morning, knowing that if Ben was struggling with any outside stresses such as money or girlfriend troubles, Casey would probably know about it.

The obligatory shelves of law books in her chambers gave the room a library-like feeling, and Janet wished she had an easy chair and a roaring fire instead of the arid, modern office furniture that surrounded her. As she reached up to dislodge a large book of evidence law, she was aware that her short stature had some consequences, among them needing assistance to get to things she wanted. On the other hand, it meant that she was able to date and dance with all the boys in high school since, unlike some of her friends, she didn't dwarf anyone on the dance floor.

As she made herself as comfortable as possible in a faux leather arm chair, she mused about the need for research in a criminal case. Most trials relied on established rules for procedure and evidence. There was also the cushion of appellate opinions on close questions of law and judges often relied on prior cases and other judge's reasoning to provide guidance. Still ,this was state court and the use of expert testimony was not a regular occurrence, other than testimony from their labs and other investigative agencies. But experts would be plentiful in the dog case and the *Florida Rules of Evidence* contained limited scholarship on the qualification of experts prior to trial. They did, however, set forth the basic requirements, and they provided references for the more subtle questions that might be raised in a contentious dispute. It was not insignificant in a case such as *Diemert*. When a case involved new or developing legal theories, it was expected that there would be what was known in trial parlance as "the battle of the experts." These battles had become common in complex civil litigation involving environmental law and medical malpractice. They were less likely to arise in criminal cases, but the "Dogicide" trial, which was finally under way, would require that she rule on whether each side's expert witnesses were qualified to give opinions on the critical question of whether a pit bull could be trained to kill a human being on command.

Although expert testimony could be long and boring, it was frequently the thing that juries relied on most. Each of the parties in the *Diemert* case had no less than a dozen experts listed to testify. She was deep into the chapter on qualifications when Berthina opened the door.

"Girl," Berthina said in her best "down home" patter, "you are gonna be looking up at the green grass if you don't get a real life."

Janet had long ago made it clear to people that calling her "girl" was not okay. Berthina was an important exception to the rule. It was past time to leave, and Berthina's caution was appropriate to the hour and to the fact that Janet had no life outside of court. Rubbing her midsection to ward off the pain that occasionally gripped her without any apparent reason, she stood, checked her pockets for her car keys, and called over her shoulder, "I'll go look for that real life."

She was about to find it—and a hell of alot more.

|21|

THE AISLES AT Target were crowded with evening shoppers looking for the latest bathing suit, tank top, or sandals. The clothing that some hapless employee had neatly and carefully stacked on tables according to size and color was now in shambles, pulled apart by impatient bargain hunters and by seasoned sorters who knew instantly what was worth looking for in the piles and what was not worth their time or trouble. A large sign hanging from the ceiling announced the checkout line.

"I'll meet you at the checkout in exactly fifteen minutes," Casey said as her eyes moved expertly across a table of shorts in khaki and white cotton.

Luke stood beside her, looking more like a padded

statue of Everyman than a live person. His normally expressive face was inscrutable, and out of uniform, he seemed to lose some of his commanding presence. As if understanding this, he shrugged his shoulders in an exaggerated gesture of resignation and looked briefly at his watch before planting himself in the nearest chair. *Fifteen minutes, my ass!* he thought. Although he enjoyed the idea of developing a serious relationship with a woman like Casey, admittedly nice-looking and incredibly smart, he despised the roles he was apparently expected to assume. Wasn't this the age of emancipation for men as well as women? Couldn't he assert his inalienable right to watch a Marlins game instead of a lot of overweight women dragging snot-nosed kids through a store? He was reaching for his phone to check for messages when it went off in his hand. A quick look at the screen told him that this was not a social call. It was understood that he was to be contacted only in the event of a serious emergency. A call from central division operations meant either a crime in progress that required extra assistance or a homicide that called for all hands on board.

When Luke heard the operator's words, he didn't move a muscle. No one looking at him would have guessed that his heart rate had just gone up twenty points. He took off without a glance behind him, not giving a moment's thought to Casey or her confusion or distress when he failed to meet her as promised. He had only one thought on his mind: find the son of a bitch who had murdered and mutilated Benjamin Toledo.

22

THE INSIDE SEAM of Harold Cohen's trousers was damp, and a slow itch was spreading down his inner thigh. He tried to stand with his legs farther apart, hoping to air-dry the moisture or at least to feel it less. His face showed none of his discomfort; nor did his somewhat combative posture signal the terror he was experiencing standing on the landing of one of Detroit's most decrepit buildings, in one of its most dangerous neighborhoods. What had once been a clearly checkered black-and-white linoleum floor was now a scarred and torn surface revealing slices of the cement and wood strips beneath. Amazingly, the carved wood on the cornice above the door as well as the moldings still retained some of the look and smell of grander times, an era more elegant than its current incarnation as a walk-up mosque.

Harold was about to turn and bolt down the steep stairwell when a short and wiry black man appeared suddenly beside him. Harold had not heard him come down from the higher floor, and as he viewed the man's amused expression at Harold's distress, it was clear that this surprise was no accident.

"So, man, you looking for some help?"

"Some help?" Harold repeated, feeling more and more out of his depth, despite the fact that he was nearly a foot taller than his inquisitor.

"Don't play with me, Jew boy. You got twenty seconds to tell me who, where, and how much—and if not, then I'm just your bad dream."

Shit, Harold thought, *it's been fifty years since I heard that racial slur.* The itch in his crotch was now so severe that he was tempted to turn away on some pretext, just to give himself a chance for a quick and rough scratch at it. But his new friend moved his stare from Harold's face to the landing below them and he disappeared up the next flight of stairs as quickly and silently as he had arrived.

It's just as well, thought Harold, his courage long gone. The former FBI agent who had recommended this kid had a history lower and darker than the basement of this dilapidated building. Harold knew he could do a better job of finding someone to kill Josiah Diemert if it turned out that the bleeding-heart judge found a way to give Diemert a break.

When Harold arrived at his Bloomfield Hills home, a traditional Georgian complete with pillars and a circular driveway, he chuckled to himself about his earlier encounter. "Jew boy, my ass!"

PUNISHMENT

His good mood fled quickly as he opened the door and heard the sound of Miriam's sobbing. It was endless, this suffering. And what, he asked himself for the umpteenth time, what in God's name had they done to deserve this?

23

THE ELEVATOR TO the parking garage had been the butt of endless jokes since the new Justice Complex first opened. Some of the staff referred to it as the "Roving Ritz," while others preferred the "Taj of Tragedy." Finished in elegant gray-and-white granite and sleek stainless steel, it looked more like a private ride to a penthouse apartment than a place to ferry judges up to their chambers and courtrooms. Still, the special elevators did immunize the judges from mingling with witnesses, attorneys, police, and the wives and children of defendants, who often attended trials where their loved ones faced serious jail time if convicted. Janet would have liked to remove these children, whose presence was partly to arouse sympathy for the defendant during trial and, at sentencing hearings, was aimed at her with the hope that she would see the impact of a jail sentence on an entire family. In fact, the reports prepared by the probation department prior to the sentencing date provided all the information the judge needed regarding the contribution of the defendant to the family's well-being and income, a contribution which was too often nonexistent.

Janet was not surprised that she was the only rider on the "Taj" that night. Most court personnel worked a normal day and, when necessary, extended their hours by arriving earlier rather than staying late. That was especially true at this time of the year, when the daylight lingered well into the evening hours, and when the endless list of fairs and parties made every night a party night. Since Stuart's death, however, Janet didn't mind working late, and she looked forward to getting home when there was only a short space of time to endure alone before her bed and an Ambien beckoned to her. Tonight was no exception, and as she stepped off the elevator into the parking garage, she was surprised by her sudden sense of vulnerability.

Oh, for heaven's sake, she thought, *they've really gotten to you. Ridiculous!* She began the long walk toward her car at the end of what was now a long row of empty parking spaces. When she caught the movement out of the corner of her eye, she stopped and, without thinking, said loudly, "Hello. Is somebody there?"

No answer. Her breath was coming quickly now, and she could feel her heart pounding against her chest. She thought briefly about turning back toward the elevator and rejected that idea. She was midway between the elevator and her car, and turning around now meant turning her back on whatever danger might be by her car.

Panicked, she decided to try something she had seen

in a movie as a child. She briefly looked over her shoulder and shouted to someone not in view, "Give me just a minute, Berthina, and I'll get the car and pick you up by the door."

She began to hum loudly as she moved toward the car, praying that this was all nothing more than her overactive imagination. Just steps away from the Camry, she heard a thud, and forgetting her earlier instinct, she began running back toward the elevator, not even looking behind her. Her breathing had completely stopped, and she suddenly knew she was going to pass out. "Help me, somebody!"

The words were expelled in a burst of air as she went down hard on the concrete, just as Stuart had done years before at Dunkin' Donuts. He was her last thought before the darkness came.

24

CASEY ARRIVED AT the Justice Complex only a few minutes after Luke had come roaring to a screeching halt at the entrance to the parking garage. Lights were flashing everywhere, but the sirens had not reached hearing distance yet. The ramp into the garage was already blocked with a half-dozen police cars, and Casey's attempt at getting past them was met with failure each time she tried. She had no idea what was going on, only that the dispatcher at police headquarters, a former college classmate of Casey's, had finally relented and told her there was an emergency at the courthouse.

As she stood behind the quickly assembled yellow-tape police line, the Rescue Squad vehicles came around the corner, and now the sirens were deafening. Casey decided to abandon her attempts to get into the building through the garage, and she ran around the block, toward the front entrance. Swiping her key card, she raced toward the elevator and saw Judge Spellman stepping in. Casey's arm banged hard against the rubber door strip, and the elevator door slid back as she slid in.

"What in God's name is going on?" she asked Judge Spellman. Suddenly realizing it was the judge, she added, "Your Honor, sir."

"I don't have all the facts yet. I do know we have one homicide and possibly two. I assume you know that Judge Kanterman may be one of them."

When the elevator doors reopened, a crazed-looking young woman came tearing across the garage, screaming, "Please, no, please don't let it be true, please, please, please!" Casey arrived at the edge of a growing crowd of police and court personnel and tried desperately to wedge her way through the crowd. No one was giving an inch. "Coming through!" she yelled in her most official-sounding voice.

"Lady, I don't know who you think you are, but you ain't coming through here," said a burly cop standing directly in front of her and talking over his shoulder.

Wanna bet, buster? Casey thought as she moved like a quarterback through the cop and a reporter standing next to him. With only a small group of people still in her line of sight, she shifted toward the garage wall. It was a good thing she did, because not a second later she was puking her guts out in the corner. She had the most ridiculous thought: how tricky it was to vomit and sob at the same time. By now Casey was on her knees, facing the wall, and she didn't trust herself to stand—not if it meant looking at her friend Ben's body again.

As she dug in her pocket, searching for anything to use to wipe her mouth, she felt an arm coming from behind and lifting her up. She knew it was Luke before she saw him. *What is there,* she wondered, *about the touch of someone you love that makes you recognize it immediately?*

"Go home," he said in a tone that made it clear that it was an order, not a request.

"But what about the judge?" Casey looked up at Luke, afraid to leave without knowing and equally afraid to get the answer.

"I can't talk about that now, Casey. I'll see you at home. Later—much, much later."

Luke turned and walked through the knot of people, and against her better judgment, Casey looked again at Ben's body. The back of his head and neck were covered with blood. She couldn't see his face, thank God, but the body was hanging from the door handle of Judge Kanterman's Camry by a leather leash—a dog's leash. And around Ben Toledo's neck someone had fastened a sharp-toothed training collar. Feeling the bile rising in her throat again, Casey followed Luke's orders and ran toward the garage ramp and exit.

"Damn this fucking dog case!" It hadn't yet occurred to her that she also might be out of a job.

|25|

BRITTANY MCGINTY LOVED her Uncle Jack. She knew that a lot of the family would have nothing to do with him. They didn't mind his drinking so much. They were Irish, after all. But they were tired of bailing him out of trouble. Her aunt and her mother would stand around the kitchen telling horror stories about his escapades as a young man. They joked about the number of bastard children who might someday come knocking on his door looking for a little help from "Daddy."

"Used to be," said Aunt Marie, "they couldn't prove a thing. But now, bang, they're giving a drop of blood and getting a lot of mileage and child support to boot."

But Brittany liked Uncle Jack's stories about his parents

and the old days in the neighborhood. He always singled her out at family picnics, and when she was ten, he would let her take a sip from his drink, which looked just like Dr. Pepper in its icy, tall glass. Given her gene pool, it was pure luck that she couldn't stand the taste of alcohol. Besides, Brittany read every fashion and fitness magazine she could lay her hands on, and nothing that was loaded with all those calories was getting past her lips!

She didn't see a lot of Uncle Jack, but she was tickled that he had a smartphone and that he knew how to text on it. Most people his age couldn't call Information on their cell phone, let alone send silent messages over the Internet. He didn't always answer her messages, especially if they were about some Hollywood gossip. But he was really grooving on her texts about the trial.

She was able to text messages to a lot of her friends and contacts during the endless hours of downtime during the trial. The interruptions were infuriating. Somedays it felt like Sunday Mass: first they sat down, and then they were up. No one had asked them yet to kneel, but the jurors kidded among themselves that they felt like puppets. They would exchange knowing looks every time there was a heated argument between the lawyers. If the judge couldn't work it out right away—bam!—the jury was sent out of the court-room again.

It was during one of these breaks when the jurors were on their way to lunch that Brittany overheard an argument between the judge and the very tall thin young man who worked at the court. She was pretty sure the guy was an underling, but he was really mouthing off to Judge Kanter-man. She hadn't heard everything, but the young guy was complaining about looking through a bunch of files to find something the judge wanted to see. *What the hell was that about?* she wondered.

As she headed out toward North Dixie, she remembered that Uncle Jack had seemed interested in this case. She brought him up to date about everything, including the argument with the judge. Uncle Jack was a stickler for manners, and he'd be surprised that a kid would talk that way to a judge. She tapped the "send" button and dropped the phone into her purse. It hummed almost immediately with Uncle Jack's reply: "Tell me more!"

Brittany was thrilled by the instant message. Uncle Jack was now officially part of the high-tech generation. She might even teach him to tweet the next time she saw him.

26

CASEY HEADED STRAIGHT for the refrigerator when she got home. If she'd ever needed a glass of chilled wine, it was now. Her hair was pulled back in a rubber band, and she yanked it free, hoping it might relieve the throbbing in her temples. She hadn't seen a lot of dead people before; in fact, her Uncle Timothy had been the only corpse she had seen up close. Although her family was Catholic, nobody except Uncle Tim's family had wanted a wake. In fact, much to the dismay of the more pious relations, several of her relatives had opted for cremation.

"Jesus! I've got to clear my head of this horror show." She headed toward the bedroom, thinking about a long, hot bath and maybe a cup of tea later. When she heard the front door lock turn, she had a reflexive moment of panic and then realized that it must be Luke, who had been her on-again, off-again roommate for nearly a week.

Still, it seemed odd that he hadn't called out to her. After all, it was her house. She slid into her terrycloth robe and opened the door tentatively. Relief wasn't the only thing she felt when she saw him. Luke was leaning against the mantle above the fireplace, and although his hand covered his face, the movement of his shoulders made it clear that he was sobbing. Casey didn't move a muscle. She felt like an intruder—a voyeur. It seemed like a very long time before Luke raised his head and looked directly at her.

"We need to talk," he said, motioning toward the sofa. Casey took a step backward toward the bedroom.

"Nope," she said almost flippantly, as though she could change this whole dynamic by being just as light about it as he was somber. Luke just stared at her. Neither one of them moved.

Casey wasn't even conscious of the tears running down her cheeks and onto her bathrobe. But Luke was, and, still silent, he came to her and drew her head down to his shoulder.

"Ben's dead, of course. You already knew that. Judge Kanterman is in critical condition. She apparently had an abdominal aneurysm that finally blew under the stress. She bled a lot internally, and she's not young."

Casey felt like she was floating. She heard every word that Luke spoke, but she didn't seem to register any of it. She pulled back and looked in his face. He was suffering too.

"Who?" she asked, "Who the fuck would do this? Ben Toledo wouldn't hurt a fly. This is sick, sick, sick!" She began stomping around the tiny room while she shouted at the walls, the ceiling, anything at all.

She didn't expect Luke to have any answers, and he didn't. Exhausted, she fell onto the couch and stared up at him with her tear-stained, mascara-smudged face.

"Casey, I'm not good at speeches. Not my style. But you need to get it together. Judge Kanterman was smack in the middle of a very notorious trial, and whether she lives or dies, this case has to go forward. It won't just disappear—and you can't either."

"What judge is going to be willing to take this case?" Casey asked. "Can they change the venue again?"

Luke shook his head. "I'll be damned if I know what's going to happen now. I'm no lawyer, but I'm sure they can't just take a walk. It's not my problem. Ben is my problem. The bastard who killed him is my problem. Our failure to see this coming is my problem." Casey jumped when his fist slammed down on the glass cocktail table, sending a crack running from the edge to the table center.

"Oh, God, Case, I'm sorry."

Casey looked indifferently at the table, hoping it wasn't the only thing broken for good.

27

THE STORY BROKE too late for the dailies, and most of the jurors left home early for the courthouse, so the groans were audible when Casey, wearing sunglasses to cover her swollen eyes, came into the jury room to announce that the trial could be postponed until the following day or perhaps two days.

"What the hell is going on?' a black woman asked indignantly, evidently feeling unappreciated by a system that pulled her off a job that she didn't dare lose and paid her a lousy fifteen bucks a day for the privilege.

Casey raised her hands like a thief caught red-handed. "I am so sorry, people. This is something completely beyond our control. The judge is very ill, and everything has happened so suddenly that everyone and everything is up in the air."

The young woman who had caught Casey's eye during jury selection raised a well-manicured, deeply tan hand. "Do we have to show up every day, or can we go back to work and forget about all this?" Other people nodded and hummed in agreement.

"Judge Spellman is meeting with some court personnel right now, and he'll be coming down to talk to you shortly. As far as going back to work, that really depends on what's decided in these meetings, so we'll just have to wait."

"Well, that's all we do anyway, honey," said an older man standing at the back wall near the jury's private bathroom. "Mind telling us what the entire police force from the State of Florida is doing here for a judge who got a little sick? Damn, I hate this bullshit!"

Before Casey could answer, the door opened, and Judge Spellman came into the room, followed by Chief Anderson. Everyone shuffled into a state of quiet alertness as Judge Spellman began to address them.

"These are very difficult times for all of us. As you will no doubt learn when you leave this room, one of the bailiffs for our court was apparently the victim in a homicide in our parking garage. I have no details about this crime. I know no more than the news media, and probably a good deal less." Judge Spellman turned to the Chief standing on his right. "Chief Anderson is leading the investigation into these events, and they do not impact you directly.

"However," he continued, "Judge Kanterman's very serious medical condition has an immense impact on you and on this trial, and we have been meeting to discuss various possibilities for dealing with the situation."

"Mistrial," muttered a middle-aged woman standing near Judge Spellman.

"That is incorrect, madam," said the judge. "The law

requires a mistrial in only a limited number of circumstances, and only when one or both of the parties request it. None of these is applicable here. In fact, contrary to what you may have been told, the work on this case—your work, I might add—will continue later today, following the noon recess. In the meantime, remember the admonition you received from Judge Kanterman. You are to speak to no one about this case until you are told otherwise. Is that clear?"

There was a chorus of agreement. It didn't include Brittany, who was seated at the table well out of Judge Spellman's line of vision, and who was busily texting everyone interested in this case, especially Uncle Jack. His reply was short: "Keep me posted, Brit. Out of town for a while."

28

"I DID NOT fucking count on this!" He was screaming and pounding on the steering wheel as he drove wildly toward the Keys. "Fuck, fuck, and fuck!" The ancient Nissan Maxima held the road easily, but Jack McGinty was way too out of control himself to appreciate good engineering. He badly needed a drink. Anything would do at this point, but to reach the small almost empty flask in the back seat meant pulling to the side of the road—always a mistake here in the Everglades. The goddamn highway police thought anyone not trailing a boat or sporting searchlights to catch a glimpse of a wild bird must be a terrorist or a poacher, and being stopped was definitely not on Jack's agenda.

So he drove and tried to focus on a plan. When he had come roaring out of the Justice Complex's parking garage, he was shaking so badly that he had trouble holding onto the gearshift. Nothing had prepared him for the violence. His business partner had called him in the early evening, just as he returned from what he hoped would be one of his last AA meetings for a while. "We need to make an impression on some people. I'll be at your house in five minutes. We'll take your jalopy. And for chrissakes, don't leave your house lights on. This isn't a first date."

As they had driven toward the Justice Complex, Jack began to lose his nerve, even though his buddy assured him that this was a little prank to spook the judge and take her mind off other matters, like a certain missing journal entry for Jack's hit-and-run conviction. "This is for you, shithead," he spat as he pulled into the alley behind the building.

Jack was amazed at the ease with which they entered the building. Where the hell was security? On the other hand, almost everyone of importance had left hours ago, and they could easily be mistaken for maintenance workers in their jeans and T-shirts. Jack was looking over his shoulder constantly, expecting someone to bring him to his knees with a hard blast to the back of his head. His fear was so great that he felt pins and needles moving over his scalp.

Ben Toledo was waiting just inside the double glass doors to the security corridor. He motioned for them to follow him to the jury room near the end of the hall. Jack's sidekick moved in two long strides, up into Ben's face. They were almost the same height, and Jack was feeling like a dwarf in their midst. "Jesus, man, what's up with you? I don't need any more stuff, and I sure as shit don't need you hanging around here." Ben reached in his pocket and, peering over the other man's shoulder, fixed his gaze on Jack. "Here's the disc. Take it, and get the fuck out of here."

Ben had dropped the disc on the large table used by

jurors during breaks and for their deliberations. He was walking quickly around the table and toward the door when he was tackled to the ground. "Son of a bitch! You must think I'm really stupid. How would I know that this is the disc we need? Get up, asshole." Ellis pulled on Ben's shirt until they stood eyeball to eyeball.

As Jack replayed the scene again and again in his mind, he couldn't understand why Ellis Watson smashed his fist into Ben Toledo's face before Toledo even had a chance to answer him. But he did—and the kid fell backward into the jury room bathroom and just about shattered the sink as he landed on it with his head and upper body. One thing was certain: Ben Toledo had smashed his head on the hard, cold, white porcelain with the force of a linebacker.

It wasn't every day that Jack McGinty wet his pants. But the piss was running before he heard Ellis pleading with Ben to open his goddamn eyes. It didn't take long to figure out that the skinny kid was dead, but it felt as though he and Ellis had stood around for hours. It was actually the sound of a vacuum that brought them back to reality.

Ellis sounded hoarse as he turned to Jack. "There's a private judge's elevator down to the parking area. You fuckin' stink, man. Jesus! Never mind—just grab his legs, and go toward those double doors." Ellis was breathing in gasps, his words exploding like small firecrackers.

"What about the dog collar? Aren't we going to leave it on that judge's desk? Wasn't Ben gonna do that?"

"Never mind that. Put it in your pocket. We don't have time to scare the stupid judge." Ellis was pulling Ben's body by the armpits. Jack, holding the dead man's feet, was feeling increasingly lightheaded and wanted to drop the body and run as fast as he could.

They found the elevator just where Ellis said it would be. When the doors opened a small chime sounded, and both men froze. They could still hear the sound of the vacuum, and now they heard voices in the distance as well. Some broad called out, "I'll go look for that real life."

"I've got an idea about that dog collar," Ellis said, as the elevator reached the ground floor. Walking backwards, he pushed open the doors into the judges' garage and moved toward the only car that remained, a Camry in the last space. As he struggled to carry the body, Jack noticed that his piss wasn't the only foul odor coming from their little group as it plodded across the cement floor. "Get him by his knees, man," Ellis hissed. "You're giving me no fucking help here."

By the time they reached the car, Ellis was sweating like a wet sponge as he tried to maneuver the body around to the driver's side of the car.

"Whoever owns this car is in for a big goddamn surprise," Ellis whispered, the hint of a smile on his face as he imagined the person's horror at discovering Ben's lifeless body. Ellis lifted Ben up and turned to Jack. "Hand me the dog collar, buddy. This may not turn out so bad after all." Jack wasn't really surprised to hear the judges' elevator doors open. Wasn't this typical of his miserable life up to now? One screwup after another. Why should this be any different?

"Move!" Ellis spat out. Jack barely had time to look back and see the dog collar attached to Ben's neck before he heard someone talking in a loud voice.

"Give me just a minute, Berthina, and I'll get the car and pick you up by the door."

Whoever you are, lady, Jack thought as they hit the loading dock and disappeared, *your friend won't be the only one who'll need picking up.*

Right again, Jack.

29

"GORGEOUS, ABSOLUTELY STUNNING. You look ten years younger." Casey saw a blur as the hairdresser whirled her around in the chair. "Just look at the back. Masterful." Casey was in no mood for Albert's verbal showboating today. She'd kept the appointment for a haircut only because she liked Albert and she knew he booked months in advance. She slid out of his chair and grabbed her purse off a hook, hoping to make a quick exit. Going to the hairdresser in the face of a friend's murder and a boss's serious illness seemed like the height of insensitivity.

Already feeling slightly embarrassed to be here at all, she was shocked when she recognized one of the jurors seated at the receptionist's desk. "D-don't I know you?" she stammered, certain that she did, but uncertain of the connection.

"Oh, hey," said Brittany, "you're the assistant judge in that horrible case, right?"

Brittany was not looking at Casey. She was busy texting, but Casey looked hard at Brittany and replied, "Well, you're close. I'm the assistant to the judge, and yes, it is a horrible case."

"Tell me about it! The doggie dude is bad enough, but I saw that guy who was murdered just a few days ago. First he argued with the judge, and then he got all sweaty and messed up, ya know?"

"You must be mistaken," Casey said in a somewhat condescending tone. "The man who was murdered was a close friend of Judge Kanterman, and they would have no reason to argue."

Casey now had Brittany's full attention. "Well, ma'am, I'm no rocket scientist, but I saw the dude's picture in the paper, and unless he's got a twin, that's the one."

As Casey reached for her wallet and pulled out a credit card, her mind raced through all the possible scenarios that could have led to a confrontation between Ben and Judge Kanterman. Nothing came to mind, and she was about to dismiss the whole conversation from her mind when she remembered Judge Kanterman leaning down to whisper in Ben's ear as she left the judges' meeting several weeks ago. Looking back, she realized that the exchange then made no sense either, especially since most communications between courtrooms were administrative, not the sort of things that would later provoke a serious argument—and certainly not one that could be overheard by anyone else, let alone a juror.

As she signed the credit card receipt, Casey tried to catch the girl's eye, but it was impossible. Never looking up from her phone, Brittany stood and started toward the back of the salon, where a neon sign announced Tanning and

Waxing—Walk-ins Welcome. *It's just as well,* Casey thought. *I shouldn't be talking to a juror on the case anyway.*

It would be one of the biggest surprises of Casey's life— that is, when she concluded that Brittany was indeed a rocket scientist or, at the very least, a keen observer of people.

|30|

HAROLD COHEN HAD attended every day's proceeding in the trial of Josiah Diemert. His wife, Miriam, had attended none. She had remained in Detroit despite the lure of better weather in south Florida. That was just as well. By the time jury selection was complete, Harold had already decided that his plan to get rid of Judge Kanterman was ill conceived and doomed to failure. The fact that his brief flirtation with hiring a killer had terrified him added to his decision to find another way to punish his daughter's killer should the State of Florida fail to do so.

This particular morning he sat in his usual seat near the double doors at the back of the courtroom. He was nearly giddy with elation at the news that Judge Janet Kanterman was off the case due to a serious illness. He was tempted to dash into the hall to call Miriam on his cell, when the bailiff came into the courtroom and asked people to be seated for an announcement. The jury was nowhere to be seen, so Harold assumed that they had been informed already. The door to the judge's antechamber opened, and a middle-aged black woman appeared and mounted the stairs to the bench. "Be seated, please," Judge Barbara Clarke said in a clear, deep voice, and the spectators, including the media, sat and waited.

"You are all no doubt aware by now of the terrible events of the last several days. My bailiff, Ben Toledo, was murdered by unknown assailants and for unknown reasons. The attack on this bright and dedicated servant of the court is monstrous, and I will assist our law enforcement personnel, as well as the federal investigators who have joined them, in any way that I am able. Added to this tragedy is the news that my colleague and my friend, Judge Janet Kanterman, is in the intensive care unit of Good Sam Hospital, and her prognosis is guarded. We all wish her a speedy recovery, not only because of information she may be able to provide regarding the night of the murder, but because she is a fine judge and an asset that this court cannot easily afford to lose."

Barbara paused to look at her audience, knowing that what she would say next would be no surprise to the media, whose access to inside information was legendary, but still hoping that the news would be well received. "At nine o'clock this morning, Chief Judge Spellman transferred *State of Florida v. Josiah Diemert* to my docket." There was a small stir in the room, but thankfully no audible gasps or groans. "Without discussing at length the decision to not declare a mistrial, I can assure you that there is ample precedent for the Chief Judge's ruling. We have a great deal of work to do here, so this trial will recommence at one-thirty this afternoon."

Judge Clarke stood and descended the stairs as Casey announced, "All rise. This court is in recess."

Harold Cohen knew nothing about Barbara Clarke except that she was a woman and she was fairly young. Both those characteristics seemed ominous to a man raised and tutored in a chauvinist home. As he stood to leave the courtroom, he noticed for the first time another spectator who looked vaguely familiar—much like a distant cousin. Knowing that such a thing was impossible, he resumed his usual place on the bench outside the courtroom door. Watching Harold leave the courtroom, Phyllis Cohen Hersch turned to her companion, an older man with a narrow ring of gray hair surrounding his very sunburned bald head. "You see. I told you he wouldn't recognize me. He hasn't seen me in almost twenty-five years, and I'm sure they don't know about the baby. You were worried for nothing, kiddo." Phyllis sat back in her place on the bench and pulled out a Little Princess lunchbox, which she carefully opened to reveal several sandwiches and a plastic bag of carrot sticks. "It's lucky little Amy didn't need her lunchbox this week. Let's eat up and call her. She should be getting ready for school right around now."

|31|

LAWYERS WHO CHOOSE to work in the criminal justice system, on either side, are a special breed. Just being smart is not enough, as it might be for a tax lawyer, and knowing the law is helpful, but that almost never carries the day. These courtroom gladiators need a sense of theater, an understanding of their audience akin to the finest actors and orators in history. And they need an ego that doesn't quit. Without the last quality, no prosecutor or defense attorney could live with the second-guessing from their friends and, of course, their critics and enemies.

Lloyd Schwartzman was a seasoned trial lawyer, not easily rattled or outmaneuvered. But even he was badly shaken by the turn of events at the courthouse, and it was definitely affecting his judgment. He simply wanted this case to be over with as quickly as possible. He and the Miami lawyers had met with their client early that morning, and Lloyd had pushed hard for Josiah to enter a plea before the trial recommenced. The Sunshine Boys, as Lloyd referred to the Miami team, backed him up, but Lloyd suspected they were just sick of West Palm Beach and wanted to return to their families and practices in Miami. It made no difference, because Josiah Diemert refused to roll—even for a felony that would allow a sentence of probation. Lloyd's only hope now was that hearing the evidence would change his client's mind about the possibility that the jury could bring in a guilty verdict for murder, or that the judge would want to give the jury a chance to consider a verdict for manslaughter.

Meanwhile, the prosecutor was in a similar fix. He was worried that the jury was tainted by the aura of violence brought about by Ben Toledo's murder and, therefore, they would draw the obvious distinction between a homicide by other humans and one that involved a novel theory about a dog. Even if that was not the case, Charlie Graham knew that this case might represent one of the best appeals in Florida legal history. Either way, a lot of people were already ragging on him for deciding not to demand a mistrial.

Shortly after noon, the attorneys met with Judge Clarke and her temporary bailiff, Casey. It was decided without much discussion that the trial would continue to be conducted in Judge Kanterman's courtroom, but that an accelerated schedule would go into place. "These jurors have been through a great deal already, and although I'm convinced they can still maintain impartiality, I do think we need to move at a faster clip than usual." Judge Clarke leaned forward and put her elbows on her desk. "I don't mean that I want to sacrifice effective representation by counsel—merely that I want shorter breaks and, perhaps, less argument between counsel over inconsequential matters. Can we all agree to that plan, at least in principle?"

Less than an hour later, the jury was in the box, and the State of Florida called its first witness. An overweight woman with bleached blonde hair and heavy eye makeup, wearing pink satin sweats, strode through the courtroom doors and toward the witness box. As she turned to take the oath administered by the court reporter, Judge Clarke saw that her jacket was emblazoned with a picture of a poodle and the words Parochial School for Wayward Puppies.

As soon as the witness was seated, the judge called for a sidebar with counsel. "Holy cow! What does this lady think she's doing here—the early show on Channel 3?"

Charlie Graham jumped right in. "I'm sorry about this, Judge, but Judge Kanterman was briefed on the problem and felt that she couldn't muzzle the witness in advance."

Lloyd suppressed a grin at the use of "muzzle" but basically agreed. "I guess it would be prior restraint of speech, but I'm not objecting. Given my sense of how this woman's appearance and style affect other people, to say nothing of her offensive antics, the defense has no problem allowing the jury to form their own opinions of this witness."

Judge Clarke simply nodded and resumed her seat, trying desperately not to communicate her disapproval of the witness to the members of the jury. The larger question was whether the jury would buy the woman's testimony as credible or the opinion of an expert. They certainly were paying rapt attention to her description of her meetings with Butch during his confinement at the dog pound.

The witness smiled at Charlie Graham, she smiled at the jury, and she positively grinned for the media. "I have absolutely concluded that this dog was a trained attack dog. He followed my commands without hesitation, including a command to bite my gloved arm."

"Objection!" Lloyd was on his feet in a flash." The witness

is not qualified to testify about training dogs to attack. Her expertise, if any, is in training dogs not to pee on the living room carpet."

The laughter nearly drowned out Charlie Graham's reply. "With all due respect to Mr. Schwartzman, Judge Kanterman spent long hours determining the qualification of experts for both sides in this case. Although she was unable to review this witness's testimony before she became ill, she had received a summary."

"Enough. This court has heard the testimony, and I would like to see counsel in chambers to give you my ruling. Court is in recess."

As Casey led the jurors out of the courtroom, she nodded to the young woman from the hairdresser's. It was a reminder that she wanted to follow up on the young woman's comments about Ben and Judge Kanterman.

"So, did you check me out?" Brittany asked as she caught Casey's eye.

"Not yet, but seeing you reminded me about that. I'm going to look into it after work today. Listen, even bailiffs can be wrong—just not often." Casey smiled and walked on toward the jury room.

Brittany felt like a junior detective. Swelling with pride, she sent Uncle Jack a text describing her triumph with the bailiff. She was thrilled to receive an instant reply.

"Good job, Brit. See if you can find out when this gal is going to stick her nose into that poor guy's business. Maybe you can offer her a few more tips. Love, Uncle Jack."

Getting praise from every quarter was a novel experience for Brittany. She liked it. It occurred to her that she could hang around after court ended and give that young woman some help finding the killer.

As things turned out, Casey would need all the help she could get.

|32|

THERE ARE CERTAIN pieces of evidence that are so disturbing that the court may exercise its own discretion in removing them from the view of the jury. Barbara Clarke had no hesitation about limiting the pictures of the victim and her injuries to those that were the least gory, but in order to make that determination, she was required to personally view each and every photograph and rule separately on each. By the time she finished, Judge Clarke was physically ill. The victim's inner arms had been torn apart, and the bones were visible in places. The room, including the walls and ceiling, were soaked in blood. The pictures of the dog were almost as frightening. Several showed Butch with his teeth bared and his muzzle stained with blood.

The state had rested its case after calling a parade of experts, some from as far away as England, to describe the breeding of pit bull dogs, their tenacity when they attack, and their intense loyalty to their trainer. Neighbors testified to Josiah's almost daily training sessions in the backyard, where he would shout "Attack!" and "Release!" as the dog clamped its teeth onto a small bush.

The intensity of the testimony was lightened only once during the state's case. Charlie Graham stood to address the court and to call his next witness, the dog warden on duty the day of the murder. The witness, with the improbable name of Roger Barker, came to the witness stand wearing a three-day-old beard, a filthy knit cap, and stained overalls. His testimony was intended to establish that the dog, which had been hidden in an upstairs bedroom after the attack, was crazed when Warden Barker found him.

"So Mr. Barker, please tell the jury how you were able to subdue the dog in order to take him into custody."

Warden Barker turned in the witness chair and addressed Judge Clarke directly. "I can't answer that question, Your Honor."

"But you must, Warden. If you do not answer, I may have to find you in contempt of court."

"Please, Your Honor. This is a trade secret, ma'am. I could lose my position if just anybody could catch a crazy animal."

Judge Clarke was about to say something, when the prosecutor suggested that the witness whisper his secret technique in the judge's ear, and if the judge thought it was important to the case, she could share it with counsel. Barbara agreed with the suggestion, and she stood and moved toward the witness box to allow the witness to whisper in her ear. The maneuver was unusual in the extreme, but it became more so when Warden Barker stood, winked at the media, and with his toothless mouth opened wide, leaned into the judge to share his trade secret. No one would soon forget the look of horror on the judge's face as the blast of Barker's breath made contact with her nose. The judge reared back instinctively, and then, with the steely discipline of a well-trained athlete, Barbara leaned in and held her position until Barker's technique was revealed to her.

Recovering herself amidst the chuckles, plus a few guffaws (including one from the warden himself), Judge Clarke asked if the state rested, subject to admission of its exhibits.

"Your Honor, the state has no further witnesses."

The smile of relief on Judge Clarke's face as she rose to leave the bench brought a fresh wave of laughter. Considering the horror and graphic violence they had all been subjected to for the last week, the lighter moments were certainly welcome.

|33|

CASEY RAN DOWN the list of recent calls on her phone, ignoring all of them until Luke's mobile number came up on her screen. They'd been together for weeks, and yet she still felt a jolt seeing his name. "Hello there, girlfriend. This is your boy toy calling. Sorry, hon, but I'm going to get to your place a little late. Don't start whatever you're thinking about without me. That goes for dinner too."

Anyone looking at my silly grin would think I'm ready for the psych ward, she mused as she locked the outer door to her office and headed across the hall to Judge Clarke's chambers. The door to the judge's office was ajar, but Casey decided that her small errand didn't warrant interrupting the judge and whoever else might be in chambers with her. Besides, this was just a wild goose chase, based on idle chatter from a girl whose greatest ambition was a perfect tan.

Ben's desk and file cabinets were identical to hers, except for the court calendar that was now in her office while she was helping Judge Clarke during the trial. Casey looked around the desktop and found nothing unusual. Ben was an avid sports fan, and he had collected hats, decals, and other paraphernalia that was spread around the desk and on top of the file cabinet. His computer was shut down, and it wouldn't do Casey any good, since she didn't know his password.

As she went to open the pencil drawer, Casey was surprised to find it locked. That was unusual, since nothing of importance was kept in most bailiffs' desks. She knew that the lock could be popped by reaching a button under the kneehole, a safety net for absentminded bailiffs who would otherwise be unable to get to the files needed by the court.

The pencil drawer had a slot with a dozen or so No. 2 pencils, probably kept around for jurors to complete questionnaires. The usual assortment of mints, scrap paper, and highlighters was there, along with a CD marked in Ben's hand "JM." Casey held up the disc, wondering whether it was personal or court-related. There was no other identification, and she went to replace it in the drawer.

"Can I help you with something, Casey?" Judge Clarke looked more than a little peeved at finding Casey behind Ben's desk.

Casey moved quickly to the side of the desk, still holding the disc. "I'm sorry to disturb you, Judge, but . . . actually I loaned this disc to Ben. It's my favorite group, and since it's the original, I thought it would be okay if I took it back." Casey was sure her face was bright red. She also knew that she and Judge Kanterman often joked about how easy it was to determine when a witness was lying.

Judge Clarke apparently was not in the mood to worry about Casey's credibility. "In the future, I'd appreciate it if you would check with me before you come over here and take anything." Without waiting for an answer from Casey, the judge went back into her office and closed the door.

Casey was in her car and headed home before she allowed herself to think about the implications of taking the disc from Ben's drawer. She briefly considered tossing the disc out of the window and simply forgetting about it. But her contact with the juror from the beauty salon still nagged at her, and she found it impossible to curb her instinctive curiosity. Besides, if Ben had been in some kind of trouble, and that appeared increasingly likely, she wanted to know about it, because whatever it was, it was still out there.

|34|

JUDGE CLARKE'S HUSBAND, Ellis, was no stranger to the bars that lined Clematis Street, the main meet-and-eat street in West Palm Beach. He was not a drinker, but he was a born party animal. He rarely invited the kind of trouble that would make folks stand up and take notice of him, and he was painfully aware that his good life (and his electric blue Porsche Carrera) came from his wife's pockets. On those rare occasions when he became the subject of courthouse gossip, his peccadilloes were dismissed as the misbehavior of an emasculated man. Ellis did nothing to discourage that perception, certainly nothing as drastic as getting a job. He enjoyed his freedom, and despite some lingering hints of disapproval he sensed from others, he knew that people liked him.

This afternoon, however, Ellis was in a foul mood. His life had been trucking along smoothly until he hooked up with Jack McGinty. His relationship with Ben Toledo, and his support for Ben's unfortunate addiction to Vicodin, had been a positive development for him. When Ben confided to Ellis, after a night of revelry at the court Christmas party, that he had become hooked on painkillers after an auto accident that shattered his knee, Ellis was not only sympathetic but also offered to help Ben with his supply of pills. God, but the kid was so fucking grateful! So much so that he readily agreed to provide Ellis with daily digests of Judge Clarke's whereabouts and schedule, information that allowed Ellis to make his own plans without fear of discovery or confrontation.

But Ben's biggest favor, and the one that had caused the young bailiff great mental anguish, was "fixing" the sentence for Ellis's partner, Jack McGinty. The pills were important to Ben, and McGinty was important to Ellis—critically important. The hookup place for the drugs he supplied to a small but very generous group of clients was a remote beach cabana near a resort on Key West. The location was anything but ideal, since some bridges along the narrow strip of land that made up the Keys were single-lane roads, requiring that trips from West Palm take place before dawn to avoid traffic delays. It was definitely a drive that one man going one direction could do alone, but the round trip was too tough, and a small slip-up on the return leg could mean disaster. For better or worse, Jack McGinty was a willing accomplice, a good driver, and unlikely to steal from Ellis, since booze, not pills, was his drug of choice.

"Hey, man, how you doin'?" The solid wood door of the restaurant gave way to a spacious room filled with cloth-covered tables and a long and impressive bar. Ellis didn't bother to answer. He scanned the ruby leather barstools and moved rapidly toward the rear. As he slid onto the backless stool, he said nothing to the man seated on his right and instead stared ahead at the lighted glass shelves with dozens of bottles carefully arranged to tempt even the most determined teetotaler. An attractive brunette, looking more like a gym teacher than a bartender, approached to take his order.

"Dewar's on the rocks, and spare me the fruits and vegetables." He waited patiently until his drink was served and then turned to the man seated on his right.

"My co-worker has decided to vacation in the southern provinces for a spell. Some well-earned rest, ya know?" The silence was unnerving. Ellis turned his attention back toward the mirror. Even now, even when he sensed he was in the worst trouble of his life, he couldn't help admiring his good looks.

He could see the other man's face in the mirror, his lips moving almost imperceptibly. "The fucking disc was a blank, Ellis. Get the original. Our supplies are frozen until you do. That means pissed clients, important clients who can hurt all of us. Are you hearing this, boy, or do I need to send you home to your mama in little pieces?" The husky, well-muscled man was in his fifties, an old man for these games, and the instant response in Ellis's gut was to take the guy down for the insult. But despite the man's age, Ellis knew better than to mess with him. They'd had only sporadic contact at exchange points for pills and money, but he had learned plenty about this goon from friends on the street. None of it was comforting.

"Consider it done." Ellis hoped the confidence in his voice didn't betray the nausea he felt remembering the last message he had from Jack before he lost contact with him. Something about a bailiff looking for the disc. If there was any truth to that, this whole fucked-up thing could blow up in their faces.

The meeting was over. That was obvious as the mob man slid off his stool and walked away. Ellis was taking in gulps of air to push down the rising bile when he heard a hoarse whisper in his ear.

"See you at court, asshole."

Ellis turned back toward the bar. Just the mention of court made him breathe harder, and this bullshit gang-talk was getting on his nerves—that is, what was left of them. He slammed a ten-dollar bill on the bar. The fucking disc was still somewhere at the courthouse, and he needed to find it before someone else did.

35

ELEANOR AND PHIL Portman had everything life could offer in America's playground. They had a pair of nice children, a pair of Chrysler town cars, a pair of best friends, and a complete absence of opinions about politics, sex, life, and religion. They measured their days in periods of work, play, and family. If it ever occurred to them that their own daughters seemed to find their lifestyle offensive, they dismissed it as the intemperance of adolescence.

In fact, their older daughter, Casey, had never voiced her disapproval of their materialism and superficiality. She rebelled instead. When the school ran out of detention slips and teachers felt guilty about calling in her parents for yet another conference, the principal set up a small desk outside his office and made that "Casey's Place." And that was just elementary school. Decades passed, and Casey's parents remained unchanged and beloved by all who knew them—and their eldest daughter learned to channel her energy and strong opinions about taboo subjects away from efforts to provoke her parents and toward a more receptive audience made up of friends and, especially, her younger sister, Margot.

The fact that the two sisters agreed on nearly everything in this world was only one reason that they spoke almost daily. It took a national disaster to interfere with their interest and support for one another and, especially, their willingness to share the most private information about their friendships, dates, and sex lives. Until recently, the sex part had been a one-way conversation—all from Margot.

"I'm serious! This is absolutely for real, not made up, not a spinster fantasy." Casey shifted the cell phone from one ear to the other. Either Margot was jealous of Casey's newly minted sex life or she just wanted to hear more details. "Do you remember that book about women who can have multiple orgasms? I thought it was just another test for girls to fail. Damn, was I wrong!"

Casey stepped into the elevator and reached out to hold back the door. "Got to go, little sister. Try to get a grip on the envy thing." Casey let the door close, ending the conversation. She was startled to see someone behind her and stepped back against the side wall of the enclosure. When the doors opened, she made a beeline to Judge Clarke's chambers and, looking over her shoulder, felt a stab of apprehension seeing the heavyset middle-aged man following her.

The door to Judge Clarke's chambers was closed: not unusual this early in the morning. Nevertheless, Casey rapped twice on the door; hearing nothing, she took her key and opened the door so that the judge could go directly to her desk. This was standard procedure in judges' chambers, but Casey still felt a little uneasy since her conversation with Judge Clarke about not looking at the court's files or other papers. She thought about the disc sitting on her kitchen counter and decided to return it unread to Ben's desk drawer. She felt guilty about invading his privacy and wrote herself a reminder note ("Return disc") on a small piece of paper and left it on her chair, where she would be sure to see it before she left for the day.

The man from the elevator had apparently gone toward Judge Kanterman's courtroom, since he had disappeared from view. As soon as Judge Clarke appeared, they would both head across the hall together. The State had rested its case, and everyone was curious to know whether the defendant would take the stand today. Casey had listened to Judge Clarke explain to the jurors that a defendant's right to remain silent was sacrosanct, and not only was the prosecutor prohibited from commenting on that decision, but the jurors were specifically instructed that they could not draw any conclusions from the defendant's choice. In practice, it was highly unusual for a defendant to take the stand. Although the desire to tell his or her version of events was often powerful, the certainty that they would be cross-examined by the prosecutor was an equally strong and per-suasive deterrent.

Casey looked up as Barbara Clarke came briskly through the door and headed straight toward her office. The judge seemed agitated, and Casey hoped it was not because of anything she had done.

"Casey, I need you in here, please." Casey wasted no time going into the judge's chambers and closing the door behind her. That would explain why she didn't see the heavyset man from the elevator walk over to her desk and lift her reminder note. He was being paid well to find the missing disc, and this little Post-it might just get him a great big bonus.

|36|

JOSIAH DIEMERT DID not take the stand. Instead, the defense team called a number of character witnesses for Josiah and, incredibly, for the dog. Lloyd Schwartzman had carefully selected witnesses with little or no firsthand knowledge of Josiah and Amy's home life, or of the attack. The first witness was a co-worker at the landscape company who barely knew Josiah and who admitted on cross-examination that Josiah missed a lot of days. The second witness, a distant cousin who had visited with Josiah and Amy one summer afternoon, spoke glowingly of Josiah's love for his dog and of Amy's close relationship with the animal. Charlie Graham's cross was brilliant and devastating.

"Tell me, Mr. Hoffman, were you in the park with Josiah and Butch when the dog broke loose from his leash?"

Hoffman readily admitted he had been with the couple and their dog, not sensing the trap that awaited him.

"And is it not true that Butch attacked a small puppy on that occasion?" The witness nodded his head and was reminded by the court reporter that he must give a verbal response. "And is it not also true that Butch latched onto that puppy's head, and despite the screams of the puppy owner and Amy, the dog stayed clamped on until Josiah shouted the command 'Release'?"

Hoffman looked across the courtroom at his cousin. He now saw what was coming and would not look directly at the prosecutor. Lloyd Schwartzman held his breath, but he knew the outcome here was inevitable.

"Mr. Hoffman, I'm waiting for an answer. Must the court instruct you to answer?"

Hoffman muttered that he had heard the command from Josiah. And he volunteered that the pit bull immediately disengaged.

"Would it be fair to say that Josiah Diemert was proud of his dog's performance? Wasn't he actually preening at the evidence of how well he had trained this animal to obey his commands?"

Schwartzman's objection was fast, but not fast enough. Hoffman's head was nodding in agreement even as he squirmed in the witness chair as though someone was about to pitch a fastball straight at his head.

"Sustained. The jury will disregard both the question and the answer."

Charlie Graham sat down with the look of a satisfied man. He knew that asking a jury to forget what they had heard with their own ears was like asking a goldfish to walk: it never happened, and it never would. Schwartzman knew it too. He made a half-hearted effort to rehabilitate his witness and asked for a recess for lunch. It was time to talk about a plea bargain with the prosecuting attorney. The jury might believe that they would get this case, but nobody who understood the system was fooled. This was the last minute of the last quarter, and a smart defense lawyer knew when it was time for his client to roll for a lesser crime and a lesser sentence.

Seated in the back of the courtroom, Harold Cohen knew it too. And he knew that it was never fucking going to happen.

|37|

ANY STATE ATTORNEY who makes a deal before presenting a closing argument to the jury doesn't understand how you make a name for yourself in the legal world. You can do a brilliant opening, a razor-sharp cross-examination, and a perfectly executed series of maneuvers at sidebar, but nothing leaves an impression like a first-class, bang-up closing argument. Charlie Graham not only knew and understood this fundamental rule of the road, but he was keenly aware that the media coverage for this trial was a once-in-a-lifetime event. He wasn't about to waste this opportunity for future fame and fortune (as a defense lawyer, of course), so the call he received on his Blackberry from Lloyd Schwartzman looking for a meeting on a possible plea bargain before court resumed in the afternoon went unanswered. Instead, Graham closed the door to his office and called his wife at home. He wanted to be sure she wouldn't miss his performance today.

Downstairs, the defense team sat with Josiah Diemert at a round, metal table outside the coffee shop. The lead lawyer from Miami was pushing papers across the table and talking a mile a minute at the same time. Diemert was staring vacantly at the papers and occasionally shaking his head.

Outside Judge Barbara Clarke's chambers a heavyset man waited patiently for the young female bailiff to leave for lunch. He hoped she might go home during the break, giving him vital information about her address and living arrangements. So far, though, she had not left the judge's chambers.

And across town, in a strip mall of edgy stores selling consignment clothing, adult videos, and discount hair products, Harold Cohen was in a gun store, buying what the urban cops called a Saturday night special.

At precisely 1:30 pm, Casey emerged from the back of the courtroom and called the proceedings to order. As soon as Judge Clarke sat down, Lloyd Schwartzman asked for a sidebar. A few people groaned as the lawyers gathered at the judge's bench.

"Your Honor, we have been attempting to reach the State Attorney for the last several hours in order to discuss a possible plea agreement. He has not returned any of our calls."

Judge Clarke turned toward Charlie Graham with a knowing look. "Charles, is the state not interested in a plea in this case?"

Graham gave the judge his most engaging smile and spread his hands in a gesture of helplessness. "Nothing, Judge, could be further from the truth. However, as I'm sure Your Honor appreciates, the victim's family is adamant that this case go to the jury so that justice can be done." In fact, Charlie had made one half-hearted attempt to reach Harold Cohen to discuss a possible plea deal. He wasn't worried though. Mr. Cohen had made it clear that a plea bargain of less than a life sentence would be "over my dead body."

"Tread carefully, Mr. Prosecutor." The judge wagged her finger at Graham. "Juries have been known to acquit people in cases where the facts or the law confuse them."

Schwartzman chimed in immediately. "Precisely, Judge!"

Before Lloyd could continue, however, Judge Clarke turned back toward her chair with a curt "Let's proceed, gentlemen."

After a brief huddle at the defense table, Lloyd Schwartzman stood and announced that the defense rested. There was more mumbling from the spectators when the judge excused the jury so that both sides could make arguments about the admission of particular pieces of evidence. Though generally viewed as technical and therefore uninteresting, the decision as to whether a photograph, a transcript, an e-mail message, or any number of items will be given to jurors to consider in reaching a verdict can be pivotal to the outcome. Obviously, these were issues that were best decided out of the jury's hearing.

The break in the proceedings was also fortuitous for several other reasons: First, because Luke noticed for the second time that day the presence of a heavyset man hanging around the door to Judge Clarke's chambers; and second, because Harold Cohen devised a plan to get his gun into the courthouse.

38

THE NEWS THAT closing arguments were about to begin spread quickly through the courthouse. Several judges delayed sentencing and probation violation hearings so that they and their staff could attend. In fact, Judge Helberg took a break from making calls to lawyers to solicit campaign contributions (indirectly, of course) and came in through the jury entrance to the courtroom to snag a good seat near the bailiff's bench. A half-dozen court reporters who had worked on the case drew lots to see who would work the final day of the trial.

The members of the jury were also in a state of high anticipation. Some had already decided on the guilt or innocence of the defendant and were just anxious to get their service to their state and their country over with as soon as possible. Others were less certain of their verdict and hoped that the closing arguments would help them get a better handle on all the evidence they had heard.

Brittany was in the latter group. At the start of the trial she was firmly convinced that Josiah Diemert was guilty of murder. But as she listened to the experts and thought more about how crazy some dogs could get, she was a little less sure. Besides, she now knew that both Amy and Josiah were out of their minds that night. The coroner had testified that Amy Cohen had so much Vicodin, Percocet, and alcohol in her system the night she died that she probably felt no pain— literally. Brittany had seen Uncle Jack get pretty wasted on a number of occasions, especially at family dinners when he got into it with her mother, and she knew he really didn't mean what he said. He was always sorry the day after, and he even sent her mother flowers once. She still thought the defendant was super creepy, but what if he didn't even know what he was doing? What if he didn't mean to do anything to Amy?

Casey called court to order at exactly nine o'clock. She knew there would be full media coverage, and she had taken special care that morning to look professional. Unfortunately, that included wearing higher heels than usual, and she was already regretting that decision. As Judge Clarke was mounting the bench, Casey scanned the courtroom. She noted that a large number of court personnel had turned out to hear Charlie Graham's close. And Charlie's wife was seated in the front row, along with several of the newer members of the State Attorney's office.

Harold Cohen, Amy's father, was seated in the back row. He hadn't missed a day of the trial, and she'd bumped into him a number of times at the coffee shop or outside chambers. He was unfailingly a gentleman, and she couldn't help but feel very sorry for him. In fact, just this morning she had seen him near the garage entrance wrestling with some suitcases and a backpack. When she approached him to offer assistance, he initially declined, but on further thought, he said that he was packed to return to Detroit as soon as a verdict was reached, and had carried with him some sandwiches and cans of pop for the wait while the jury deliberated. If Casey could just take the backpack up to the courtroom, he could handle the rest.

"Glad to help, Mr. Cohen. I'll leave the backpack next to my desk." Casey swiped her card as usual, and when the scanner beeped, she shrugged and gave the deputy sheriff her winning smile. "Pop cans."

Casey checked the courtroom again, but apparently Luke was too busy to attend. That was a shame, not only because the mere sight of his face coming toward her filled her with warmth and a sense of welcome, but also because she was able to share so much of what happened at the court with him, and he understood. In fact, just this morning at breakfast, she had mentioned the disc from Ben's desk drawer and her plan to return it without downloading. She had felt a little embarrassed just telling Luke about her snooping and Judge Clarke's irritation with her. To her surprise, Luke had suggested that she hold onto the disc until one or both of them could run it and then make a decision. She had the disc in her oversized L.L. Bean canvas bag and planned to boot it up after court today or tomorrow.

As Charlie Graham stood to address the jury, Casey noticed that Josiah Diemert seemed to be paying attention for the first time in this trial. He certainly wasn't alone. The jurors were on the edges of their chairs.

|39|

"HELP ME, JOSIAH! Help me!" Charlie had raised his voice to a falsetto soprano. His arms were open in a parody of supplication. "But," Charlie said, lowering his voice, "no one helped Amy Cohen. No one came to her aid as the dog attacked—and released—and attacked—and released—and attacked—and released—again and again, on command from its owner, Josiah Diemert. This vicious animal did what it had been trained to do, did what its owner had decided in an instant must be done."

Suddenly, like an animal himself, Charlie spun toward the defense table and lowered his head toward Josiah Diemert. "That man had the power of life and death at his command. Only he could save Amy Cohen, and only he

143

could kill her using a weapon of horror—the bared teeth of a breed of dog so fearsome that many countries have banned its presence on their soil. An animal famed for its bloodlust and for its tenacity. Don't be fooled by Josiah Diemert. This was not an accident. This was not a wild, crazed animal raging beyond its owner's frantic efforts to bring it under control. It was the owner, ladies and gentlemen, who was wild and crazed. It was this defendant who had the bloodlust. It was Josiah Diemert, the man who trained this animal to always answer to his command, who killed Amy Cohen."

Josiah sat at the defense table, watching Charlie Graham's performance before the jury. He felt completely disconnected from the proceedings playing out in front of him like a daytime soap opera. The truth was that he no longer cared. They could believe whatever they wanted. Only he knew the truth of what had happened that terrible night, and even he didn't know all of it.

If he closed his eyes, he could almost taste the blood that had gushed from his lip after the glass was smashed into his face. Amy had hurled the tumbler with such force that he was amazed when he saw its dreamlike descent, unbroken, to the bedcovers. He was unclear why she had attacked him. After all, he was the injured party that day. First she had come home whispering obscenities at him, and then she'd left the house for God knows where. When she finally came through the door after midnight, she'd reeked of booze and weed. And she'd reeked of sex. He could smell the cum from the couch when she passed him, heading for the bedroom. The dog had been asleep on the floor next to him and, as always, his saliva was almost as pungent as the smells trailing Amy.

He'd asked himself a thousand times if Amy had wanted to kill him. He had a vague memory of thinking that she was going to waste him right then and there. She was screaming like a banshee, "Fuck you, asshole! Fuck you! Get down with your stupid dog, bozo! Go on and suck the rug, shithead!" He had stood at the foot of the bed, staring at her in complete astonishment. He knew she could be verbally abusive when she was high on drugs, but he'd never seen her like this before. She looked like shit—bloodstains on her uniform and a black eye from their fight earlier. But she was beat up bad now.

His gaze shifted to the nightstand where a half-emptied glass of gin sat. "Here," he had said, handing it to her. "Drink this, and calm down, you stupid bitch."

He didn't see the glass coming at him. The blood was unexpected, but then Amy had told him how incredible it was the way tongues and lips would bleed like fucking faucets. He watched the blood pour down his chin, mesmerized in part by the stupendous volume of heroin he had consumed since Amy broke away and ran that afternoon. He didn't have a memory of any pain, just the picture of the bright crimson blood dripping from his chin.

He was startled back to the present, to the courtroom, by the sense of impending danger. A finger was pointing at his face, and the reddened face of Charlie Graham was only inches away from his.

"Objection. Objection, Your Honor!" Lloyd Schwartzman was on his feet and already approaching the bench. "Mr. Graham is literally threatening this defendant. The State Attorney is out of control, Judge."

A tactic like Graham's was as risky as it gets. If the defendant's lawyer doesn't rise to the bait, but instead raises a lengthy and wordy objection, then the momentum of the closing argument will be lost. Still, Graham felt it was a gamble worth taking, especially when he looked up at Judge Clarke and said quietly, but well within the jury's hearing, "If this seems threatening to the defendant, Your Honor, I guess we can all imagine how terrified Amy Cohen was the night she was being torn apart by an animal under the direction and control of her common-law husband."

"That's enough, gentlemen. How much more do you have, Mr. Graham?"

"I'm finished, Judge, until my final closing." Charlie turned and looked meaningfully at the jury. "These fine folks have the picture."

Before the defense could object, Judge Clarke rose and raised one hand as if to stave off any further argument. "Court is adjourned until one-thirty this afternoon."

The jury, many of whom had become good friends over the course of the trial, turned in unison, looking more like a marching band than a group of very tired citizens. The State Attorney's opening close, as it was known in courtroom parlance, had left the jurors, as well as the spectators, emotionally drained. But one spectator, the middle-aged, well-dressed man in the back row, was an almost frightening sight to behold. His balled fists were pressed into his eyes with such force that the skin around his cheeks had ballooned and turned purple. Although his sobs were barely audible, the heaving of his shoulders left no one in doubt as to his agony. People filing past looked with curiosity at Harold Cohen and quickly turned away, scorched by the heat of his anger and despair.

The courtroom was empty when Casey walked out to retrieve some papers that Judge Clarke had requested. She saw a very different Harold Cohen standing as though waiting for her to appear. In keeping with his usual affable and courtly manner, he approached Casey and inquired politely about the backpack she had carried into the courthouse for him that morning.

"I'm so sorry. I completely forgot." Casey turned heel and returned moments later with the backpack. "You must have packed a meatball sub sandwich for lunch today. This is not what I'd call a light lunch."

Casey gave a few comic lifts of the carrier and handed it to Harold, who took the handle with a casual gesture that belied his anxiety. He knew that if the bag had been opened and searched, he would have a lot of explaining to do, but he would probably get by with a reprimand. On the other hand, if his motive for bringing the gun into this courtroom for this case was ever unearthed, he'd be in very big trouble. *I really don't give a good goddamn,* he thought. To Casey, he merely nodded and smiled, looking like a man in mourning who needed whatever sustenance he could lay his hands on.

Casey was right on. The small-caliber pistol was all the nourishment Harold Cohen needed for the moment. In fact, he felt sated with the sense of power it gave him as he slipped it into his pants pocket. Harold Cohen was fed by the certainty that if the jury failed his daughter, he would not.

|40|

WHEN A JUROR falls asleep during a trial, people are amused. When a judge nods off, her nap becomes the subject of criticism and courthouse humor. Barbara Clarke knew that she had come dangerously close to closing her eyes during the earlier stages of the trial, especially during the technical testimony of laboratory specialists and other expert witnesses. She had paid close attention, however, to the coroner's testimony, especially his comments regarding the levels of controlled substances in the victim's body. She had hoped that the defense team would challenge the coroner as to whether Amy Cohen was so far gone during the attack that she was basically anesthetized and felt no pain. But the coroner was allowed to testify that the victim had suffered horribly despite the presence of near-toxic amounts of Vicodin and Percocet in her system at the time of her death.

Barbara knew that one of the hazards of presiding over a criminal trial—or any trial, for that matter—was the tendency of the judge to orchestrate the proceedings in her mind, including what the attorneys should ask of witnesses and how they should argue their cases. Judges frequently shared stories of their frustration and occasional dyspepsia over the incompetence of lawyers in their courtrooms. Some judges couldn't resist the urge to "try the case from the bench." It was common knowledge that certain jurists would drop hints to one side or the other about a better trial tactic or argument. Worse still were the grimaces on the faces of some judges when a newer lawyer (or, heaven forbid, a female) made an obvious goof in cross-examination.

In this instance, Barbara was less concerned about substituting her judgment of the lawyers' performance than she was about rescuing a case that was already overloaded with reversible error. For that reason, she had already decided that if the State Attorney's office was unwilling to work out a plea with Diemert's team, she was going to recommend that the jury be given a choice of verdicts in this case—at least one of which would allow them to find the defendant guilty of a crime of passion instead of intentional murder.

It was almost time to return to court, and Barbara's look of shock at her husband's sudden appearance in her chambers was followed quickly by a frown of annoyance. She knew that Ellis had managed to snag a card that allowed him the same access to the courthouse as she had been given. It was a free pass to avoid the lines at security and to use the judge's elevator instead of the elevators used by the public at large. Barbara disapproved, but that had never meant a thing to her husband in the past. And he was not a man who tolerated inconvenience or limits.

"Jesus, Ellis, you scared me half to death. What are you doing here in the middle of the day? You know I'm in trial." Barbara stopped talking. It was clear that no one was listening, least of all her husband. She stood and moved toward the door, glancing out to see who might be hanging nearby before closing it firmly. Staring at her husband's back, she felt an overwhelming urge to push him hard, to topple him over onto her desk and experience his vulnerability. Her rage surprised and embarrassed her. She walked deliberately around him and faced him across the desk. Her instincts told her that she needed a buffer between them.

"I need your help, Barbara." He abruptly raised his hand so that the palm faced toward her. "Stop. Do not say it. Don't fucking say anything. Just nod, like you might just be a woman, like you might just be a man's wife, instead of a keeper." Ellis's voice had risen from a whisper to a near shout. He silenced himself with an angry swipe of his hand across his mouth.

She sat down heavily in the large leather chair. How was it, she wondered to herself, that she had felt this coming? A premonition of darkness crossing her path had been pressing on her since she had heard about Ben's murder. She'd wanted to see it as only part of the larger anxiety felt by everyone who had been touched by the horrific crime, but it felt personal—very personal. And now it was.

"What is it, Ellis? An underage girl? An unpaid bar bill?" She could barely hide her disgust.

He leaned across the desk, lowered his chest so that his eyes were level were hers. "Listen carefully, Barbara. Your substitute bailiff has something I need. And you're going to get it for me. She has a computer disc that was given to Ben Toledo for safekeeping, and there's a certain individual who is prepared to do all of us very serious harm if I cannot locate and deliver that disc." His sharp intake of breath was followed by a hoarse whisper. "Don't even think about asking. No cross-examination, no questions, no guesswork."

She didn't miss a beat. "You're certifiable, Ellis. I assume you're talking about Casey, and I can tell you right now that she has nothing that belonged to Ben, and even if she did, I wouldn't involve her in your scheme, whatever it is."

The sharp knock on the door could not have been timed better. Looking very much in charge of herself, Barbara walked past Ellis and swung open the door. It was a relief that no one could see the anguish on her face at that moment or sense the depth of her despair—the frustration and pain of a powerful woman who felt completely powerless to stop the train wreck that was her life.

"All rise. This Honorable Court is back in session."

41

SHE COULD FEEL the wet sand between her toes. The scratching as the tide retreated made her feel like an hourglass, locked in place as her body washed away. The shock of pain tore her apart. Looking frantically for the attacker, she leaped high in the air and hovered above the breaking waves, alert for the next intrusion.

"Judge Kanterman. Ma'am, I'm awful sorry, but I gotta roll you over to change these here sheets. I am so really sorry to pain you." The tiny nurse's aide looked unfit for her task, but she managed to skillfully turn Janet on her side, remove and replace the bottom bed sheet, and roll her back, all within the span of one loud groan from her patient. Satisfied, the aide smoothed a top sheet and would have patted

Janet Kanterman on the head as a finishing touch had not the son-in-law been seated near the window.

No one had yet given Janet's family a prognosis based on anything other than maybe and possibly or probably. Aneurysms were tricky, they all said, and although the surgery had gone well, there had been considerable blood loss. Still, it was only when her bailiff, Casey, had visited that Janet's family began to calculate the trauma of what had occurred in the garage nearly a week earlier. She had collapsed before she was found, so no one knew what she saw—or, more importantly, whom she might have seen that night. The doctors were keeping her pretty well sedated for the time being, and since the trial in the dog case was proceeding without her, no one saw any reason to cut off the morphine just to ask her questions.

Better to let her rest, her son-in-law thought. And at the time, it certainly seemed better. But a few lives might have been spared with a wake-up call.

Meanwhile, back on Wells Beach, Janet jogged in the light surf, as always counting every fourth step to gauge her time and distance. The silence of the seagulls was startling, but the scene was so rapturous that this small dissonance was flicked into the eastward wind.

42

THE JURORS WERE restless. It seemed to them that the end of the trial was taking longer than the trial itself. After the State Attorney's "first" closing argument, a number of spectators slid out of their seats and left, believing that a murder conviction was now a foregone conclusion. Some jurors watched their departure with a look of naked envy. Lloyd Schwartzman knew he had his work cut out for him, especially since Charlie would get another crack at a closing.

Lloyd always dressed carefully. His shirts were custom made, and his Zegna suits, admittedly expensive, were quiet and tasteful. Whatever time he took with his appearance, it was a fraction of the time Lloyd spent preparing for trial— especially for closing argument. He had one shot, and if he failed, his client was going to get shipped for life. He stood, straightened his Charvet print tie, and turned abruptly toward the jury box.

"So, it looks to me like you're going to find my client guilty in this case." The gasp was widespread and audible. "Well," Lloyd chuckled, "it also looks like I have your attention." Lloyd walked behind the counsel table, stood behind Josiah Diemert, and placed his hands on his shoulders.

"Something terrible happened to Amy Cohen on a warm summer night a year ago. And when it happened, this man was there. That is undeniable, and we have never denied it. Nor have we denied that the pit bull dog, Butch, was an instrument of death. So you might be asking yourself, why doesn't this fellow just sit down and let us get about our business?

"Well, I'll tell you why. It's because you can't convict this man of intentionally killing his common-law wife. If a crime was committed by a human being that night, it was a crime of passion. It was manslaughter, pure and simple."

Charlie Graham leapt out of his chair. "Objection! Objection! Your Honor, we object!" The several assistant prosecutors acting as gophers for Graham stood with him, although none of them knew what the hell all the fuss was about. Lloyd knew. The judge knew. And so did Harold Cohen.

"We'll have a fifteen-minute recess. I'll see counsel in chambers."

A few jurors shook their heads in disgust. Mutterings of "ridiculous," and "waste of time, let's get it over with already," could be heard by the deputy sheriffs near the door to the jury room. Brittany McGinty wasn't one of the complainers. She'd resigned herself to the endless waiting, and by now she openly used her smartphone in the jury room, and no one seemed to object so long as she didn't make noise. She had sent Uncle Jack a batch of text messages about the trial, but he hadn't responded to any of them. Never one for endless speculation, Brittany took a chair from the table and dragged it to a corner of the jury room, where she could text or play Angry Birds without interruption.

If some of the jurors were agitated, it was nothing compared to the attorneys gathered in Judge Clarke's chambers.

"That was beneath you, Lloyd. Damn it! I thought better of you, man." Charlie's face was red, beet red, and it was right up in Schwartzman's face. Lloyd stepped back, nearly falling over the court reporter's typing stand. Charlie reached out instinctively and grabbed Lloyd's arm.

"Hold everything!" Barbara moved through the sizeable group. "Sit down. Casey, get a chair for these other defense counsel. Okay. We're going to start this conversation by my telling you that most of what Lloyd said is not contrary to the rules. A defense attorney can always argue. Period. What he cannot do," Barbara said, turning her gaze directly on Lloyd, "is to tell the jury what the law is and what they can do that may be contrary to the judge's instructions."

Charlie didn't miss a beat. "But Your Honor, there is no charge of manslaughter in this case. In fact, it is the defense team that specifically asked the court to not give an instruction on a crime of passion."

The bickering went on, but the judge was barely listening. Her mind was on Ellis and whatever scheme he was involved with now. This was a first for them. His mistakes in the past had been just that—his, not hers. Now it seemed the toxin had found its way into her life and her courtroom as well.

She knew, of course, that Casey had taken a disc from Ben's desk drawer. She recalled vividly how embarrassed Casey had been and also how annoyed she was at the time. She wasn't about to share that information with Ellis or anyone else, but she was certainly going to ask Casey about it at the first opportunity.

Bam! Charlie's fist hit the desk, and Barbara was so unprepared that she almost levitated out of her chair. There now seemed to be a number of red faces in the room, including her own.

"This is what we're going to do, ladies and gentlemen. I am going to allow the defense to describe the events surrounding Amy Cohen's death in any way they choose, so long as they do not attempt to introduce a legal theory other than that which is before this jury at this time, and—most important—so long as the description sticks to the facts in evidence. We'll reconvene in ten minutes." Barbara looked toward the door. "Casey, please remain. I need to speak with you."

43

EVERYONE WAS ON edge. The neighboring shopkeepers, tourists and townies, including folks who didn't work at or near the courthouse could feel the tension. Secretaries, clerks, even the other judges who came to lunch counters and drugstores with searching eyes and too-rapid movements, sometimes knocking over a water glass or a salt shaker as their gaze shot from one end of a room to another as if they were in a war zone. And who could blame them? The courthouse had suffered greatly in a span of just two weeks. A bombing and a murder, and no one seemed to have a clue about who was responsible for either event, or if they were even connected.

Luke had heard all the conspiracy theories floating

around town. Someone from the clerk of courts office claimed in a voice message that her medium had absolute proof that this was retribution for the arrest of a notorious Black Panther back in the sixties. Actually, Luke's favorite was the rumor that the mother of the blind owner of the coffee shop was seeking revenge for the daily attempts to put less than the check amount into the dish on the counter, many people assuming that only blind people worked there. *Now that is a crime worthy of revenge,* Luke thought, although revenge was not at the top of his motive list. Rather, it was his assumption that Ben's murder was in some sick way meant as a diversion from something else, something important enough to trigger a bombing and a horrific killing. The evidence in the bombing case was proving absurdly elusive. Explosions, like arson fires, usually left fingerprints. A great amount of information came from the type of incendiary device used, materials employed for detonation, and location of the "spark." In the courthouse bombing, however, the preliminary investigation was providing very few clues. One fact was certain, and that was the limited nature of the bomber's intention. Had the perpetrator, an individual or a group, wanted to cause serious loss of life or damage to the building, they could have done so by adding additional fertilizer to the modestly potent bomb. This had been a well-researched, well-planned, and well-executed crime with a limited and precise objective. What exactly that objective was remained as mysterious as the identity of the bomber.

Luke had taken the unusual step of calling for federal help before they called on him. Local law enforcement was usually protective of its turf, and though the bombing alone was enough to bring the feds running, the fact that it involved a courthouse was all the more reason for them take charge. Luke had developed a great deal of respect for the Alcohol, Tobacco and Firearms division of the US

Department of Justice. The ATF had grown over the years from a small department largely focused on chasing bootleggers to one of the most respected investigative agencies in the world.

Their preliminary take on the two incidents in West Palm Beach, however, was not much help. While not dismissing the working assumptions on the ground, the two young men sent from the Miami office were mostly interested in the dog case that was proceeding in Barbara Clarke's court. They had examined the physical evidence available so far and in short order had managed to piss just about everybody off, but especially the lab people in Criminal Science Investigations by insisting that everything be shipped to Washington for review and confirmation of their findings. Luke provided whatever physical evidence his detectives had gathered, and he spent a considerable amount of time discussing possible motives and his impressions of the investigation thus far. Curiously, the ATF people seemed completely disinterested in a footprint found in the blood pooled near the place where everyone agreed Ben had either fallen onto or been hammered into the sink. Luke had discussed the footprint with the lead guy, Ken Catalano, but apparently Luke's curiosity about the size of the print, and by inference, the size of the guy with the shoe that made that print, didn't impress Catalano in the least.

Luke smiled ruefully at Casey who was seated across the table in the Pho restaurant off Fern Street. "Maybe they have more giants in the big, bad city than we do. Whoever left that bloody print is not only big, but he's light on his feet. The shoe made only a faint impression in the blood, not a deep carve from either the heel or the toe." Luke didn't look up from the clear noodles he was struggling to maneuver onto the chopsticks. His frustration was evident, and so was the toll that the investigation was taking on him. Luke's newly minted dark circles and sagging jowls were testament to his exhaustion.

But Casey's sympathy for Luke's stress was fleeting. Like so many other people at court, she wanted solutions to the crimes that had been committed right under their collective nose. She didn't like feeling unsafe at work, and she definitely felt very threatened by everything that had happened. What's more, her personal anxiety moniter was over the top for reasons she hadn't yet shared with Luke . Earlier today she had been called on the carpet by Judge Clarke over the stupid disc she had taken from Ben's desk drawer.

"Have you looked at the disc yet, Casey?" Judge Clarke was sitting on the edge of her desk, trying to look very casual. But Casey knew Barbara Clarke, and she had never, absolutely never seen this woman strike anything but a rigid and professional posture. It didn't put Casey at ease in the least. Instead, it set off warning bells.

Casey could see two options at that moment. She could lie to the judge and say that she had booted up the disc and imported the music, or she could tell her honestly that it was sitting on her desk at home, still untouched. No one could have guessed, looking at her at that moment, but it felt to Casey as though she had both grown up and lost her way at the same time.

Casey met Barbara Clarke's gaze directly. "It's not the kind of disc you look at, Judge. It's just an audio disc—you know, just the music I thought it was. I feel terrible about going into Ben's desk. I meant no harm."

Judge Clarke waved her hand dismissively. "Don't worry about it, Casey. I trust you, and it's probably not the disc I'm looking for. The disc I'm interested in has some very personal information on it, and it would be a serious invasion of my privacy if you or anyone else looked at or listened to it. In any event, I'd like the disc returned to me tomorrow morning."

Casey was hyperventilating as she headed toward the

hallway. She had lied to a judge about property that she had no right to possess, and to make matters worse, she was completely boxed in by her lie. She didn't dare look at Ben's disc now, for fear that she would discover embarrassing or harmful personal information about Judge Clarke. She couldn't give the disc to the judge, because she had no idea what was on it, but it was certainly not any music she had given Ben. And she couldn't even get help from Luke. He would be furious with her for not simply admitting to the judge that she had the disc but hadn't played it yet.

Finally, she had no words that would explain the profound sense of dread she felt about this goddamn disc and about the judge wanting it. Maybe it was a desire to protect Ben. After all, what would he be doing with something that he shouldn't have and that the judge wanted so badly? Or maybe it was just the poisonous atmosphere they were all moving in, an air pocket of fear and suspicion that no one understood or could manage.

Whatever was troubling her at work, Casey sat looking at Luke across the table and felt irritated with him. Incredibly, her anger was at him, not herself, for not sensing that she was in trouble, that she had done something dishonest, risky, and plain wrong. *I know I'm being irrational,* Casey thought to herself, *but how can he be so tone-deaf?* With her arms already crossed on the table in front of her, Casey dropped her head on them like a dead weight.

|44|

HAROLD COHEN HAD a dilemma. He had a gun in his possession—actually in his front left pocket. Clearly, he could get the weapon out of the courthouse. Security never seemed to check the departing staff and citizens. If they wanted to shoot each other outside the building, it was their problem. But getting the gun inside a second time was going to be difficult, if not impossible. After all, although Casey had a generous heart, he doubted she'd fall for the "lunch in my backpack" ruse again. And Harold was still determined to do whatever was necessary if the jury failed to do their job.

The only solution was to put the gun in a safe place overnight and almost every place he thought of had a downside.

The courtroom was out of the question. So were the restrooms and the cafeteria. Since the bombing, the cleaning crews had a security guard with them, and they were as thorough as people wished they had been in the past. The coffee shop momentarily piqued his interest, but he knew that the majority of people who worked there were anything but indifferent to their surroundings. They knew as much courthouse gossip as anyone in the building, and they came early and stayed late most days. As tempting as the back of the freezer might be, his interest would be noticed, especially since he never touched a drop of their food or drink.

When he had methodically gone floor by floor in his mind, thinking of every possibility, he finally latched onto his perfect hiding place. He bolted from the hallway bench and, like a young buck, sprinted to the double doors of the Law Library, praying that someone was still working inside. The door gave, and Harold did his best to appear nonchalant for the young man working at a desk behind the counter.

"Can I help you, sir? We're about to close up for the night."

When Harold heard the "sir," he knew instinctively that his request was likely to be granted. Wearing a suit and tie was so unusual these days that only attorneys and other professionals submitted themselves to such discomfort.

"I was afraid of that. I really need only a minute to find an article I saw here the other day. I promise to be quick."

The younger man signaled his assent by returning his attention to the book on his desk. Harold wasted no time moving through the stacks toward the one closest to the back wall and near the door marked exit. He quickly scanned the bottom shelf for the best spot.

"Sir. Sir. I'm sorry, but we really need to clear everyone out now."

Harold yanked out a book labeled *Federal Reports 3d., Volume 200*. There was more writing that he didn't understand and didn't care about. The gun, wrapped in his monogrammed handkerchief, slid neatly behind the book. He quickly pulled the adjacent books on the shelf even with *Volume 200* and stood up, just as the young man turned the corner.

"I'm all set for now," Harold called out, with a wave of his hand. He moved to the center of the aisle and strode briskly toward the doors. "See you tomorrow, then."

Funny, the young man thought as he turned the bolt on the door. He was the only one working this week, and he didn't remember seeing the older man before. And it was weird that the guy was looking through the old case reporters for an article. "Not my problem." He walked out the doors and never saw Harold in the alcove watching him depart.

|45|

HAROLD COHEN'S ANXIETY about the verdict was not
without foundation. In Harold's view, any verdict that would
allow Josiah Diemert to escape life in prison or the death
penalty was unacceptable, and he had witnessed the remain-
der of Lloyd Schwartzman's closing argument that afternoon. Lloyd's performance was masterful, even in the eyes
of the enemy.

"Okay. Let's look at the facts in evidence." Lloyd spun
around and grabbed the edge of the blackboard, the face of
which had, until now, been hidden from the jury. "There is
no evidence that my client ever abused Amy Cohen. Yes,
yes, I know a co-worker testified that Amy had a bruise or
two and had blamed her injury on a fight with her husband,

but there was no police report, and you have already been instructed that the co-worker's testimony is considered hearsay and is therefore unreliable and inadmissible. So may I repeat, there is no reliable evidence that Josiah ever hit Amy." Lloyd reached across for some chalk and with a flourish crossed out the word history.

He then tapped the next word written in capital letters on the blackboard: FEAR. "You've heard a great deal about an attempted cover-up by the defendant. Police officers have testified that Josiah told a series of conflicting stories about what occurred that night and the following morning. You've heard evidence about his pathetically obvious efforts to hide the evidence of the crime, as well as efforts to shield the dog from discovery by the authorities.

"But what you haven't heard about is the gut-wrenching fear and hysteria that this defendant must have felt on the morning after this horrible tragedy. I cannot speak for the defendant, nor can I ask you to merely speculate on facts not in evidence. But the judge will instruct you that you must use your common sense and your experiences to judge the credibility of the witnesses who have testified, and of the evidence itself. You have heard the coroner testify about the substantial amount of drugs in both Josiah's and Amy's bodies on the night in question. You have heard the police testify to the defendant's demeanor during interrogation. They used words like 'disoriented,' 'unhinged,' 'catatonic,' and 'spacey.' Are these words that describe a hardened killer, a monster who would, if you believe the prosecution, deliberately kill in an explosion of blood and gore. Is confusion a cover-up? Is disorientation a demonic device to hide the truth. Or were these fragments of stories and fantasies really just evidence of a man's hysteria and confusion?

"Finally, there is this very important word: motive. That is the elephant in the middle of this courtroom. It is the fly in the prosecution's ointment, and although the law does not require the determination of a motive for first-degree murder, common sense most certainly does!"

Now it was Lloyd's turn to spin around and point to the defendant. "Josiah had no reason to kill Amy. None whatsoever, and no one who has testified in this case has provided one to you. Oh, yes, they harp on the legal notion that intent to harm or even kill can be formed in an instant. But when that intent is formed, there must still be a motive for the act. Money is not an issue in this case. In fact, it can be argued that Amy's death was against Josiah's economic interest. Sex? We have heard repeatedly about the robust sex life these people enjoyed. Neither one had children, so there was no argument about the kids."

"Objection, Your Honor. Mr. Schwartzman is incorrect."

It was too late, of course. Like so many rising stars before him, the words had flown out of Charlie Graham's mouth before they had fully formed in his mind. There was a moment of stunned silence, as though this was the memorial service for Charlie's now defunct career. Then there was the crescendo of voices, and at its peak, the familiar sound of a gavel.

The person who banged the gavel put her head in her hands. She was beginning to regret that the bomb had not been bigger.

|46|

THERE WASN'T AN empty seat in Judge Clarke's chambers. Every attorney involved in the case was there, as was every law clerk, staff person, and deputy sheriff assigned to the judge's courtroom. There was also not a lot of conversation. No one seemed to know what to say, at least until the judge and her bailiff, Casey, entered the room.

"I don't know who wrote the script for this farce, but whoever it is has a warped sense of humor. Why don't you tell us, Mr. State Attorney, how the wheels of justice have taken this latest turn toward mayhem?"

Charlie's new navy-blue suit, purchased just days before by his adoring wife, clearly showed the wrinkles in the armpits and elbows borne of an excess of perspiration.

169

Nevertheless, he calmly walked toward the judge's desk and answered in a clear voice. "Your Honor, I apologize for the curveball. Our office became aware that Amy Cohen gave birth to a child who is living at this time with Harold Cohen's cousin in Arizona. The child was born nearly five years before Amy became involved with the defendant, and we do not know at this time if Josiah is, or ever has been, aware of the child's existence. Ma'am, we are fully aware that our state has the most liberal discovery rules in America, and we anguished over the question of whether we had a legal obligation to disclose this information to the defense. It was our considered judgment that we did not."

Barbara Clarke swung her executive-size leather chair toward Lloyd. "So quiet over here? What's your take on this, Lloyd? There doesn't seem to be anything exculpatory about the news. Nothing that would assist the defense in proving Mr. Diemert's innocence."

Charlie had remained standing next to the judge's desk. The sweat under his arms was going to ruin his new suit, Lloyd thought to himself, observing the spreading stain. "Lloyd?" The judge was now leaning forward in her seat, and Lloyd stood at his place with obvious reluctance.

"For starters, Judge, I don't know what we can or should tell the jury. Then we have the victim's family, and last but not least, the defendant himself. The cat—or in this case, the kid—is out of the bag, and even though we might manage to do more damage to the jurors, I don't see how we keep this from the others I've just mentioned."

Silence descended again on the crowded room. "Excuse me, Judge." Casey's hand was waving above the group. She was pressed against the bookshelves near the rear of the courtroom. As the people standing in front of her turned, she was thankful again for the height she'd inherited from her parents. She carefully pushed her way forward until she stood next to Charlie Graham.

"If you have a way out of this morass, Casey, let's hear it."

"With all due respect, ma'am." Barbara turned toward the source. It was one of Lloyd's co-counsel. "I don't think . . ."

He never got a chance to finish. Barbara stood behind her desk and eyed the group. "Let's start with the fact the I'm the judge, or I'm 'Your Honor,' but I am definitely not 'ma'am.' Now let's hear what my bailiff has to say."

"I simply wanted to assure you that the jurors, despite their knowledge of this case, do not understand what all this fuss is about. I have been with them during the last half hour, and their real concern is that this is just another interruption that is dragging out the trial that they definitely want to be finished."

"All right, ladies and gentlemen. I get paid to make decisions, and here is what we're going to do. First, we will make no explanation to the jury beyond my assurance that this is a legal matter. Second, the defendant will be told everything about this child that is within the knowledge of the prosecutor's office. Finally, that will be the absolute outer limit of dissemination of this information. We will not discuss this matter with the press, we will not discuss it with anyone else outside this room—and, I regret to say, that will include the victim's family. At this point it is information. It is not evidence. Should that change, I will revisit the issue."

Barbara sat down heavily in her chair. "Now, are there any more surprises I should be aware of? Or may we hope that this trial can move to an orderly conclusion?"

No one knew what might happen next. But it would be anything but an orderly conclusion.

47

CASEY'S SISTER MARGOT knew something was wrong. She had received five voicemail messages from Casey, and to describe them as frantic would be an understatement. She tried to return Casey's calls, without success, and she debated calling her at the courthouse, but she knew that Casey would disapprove of her doing so. Margot was sure that it wasn't a problem with Casey's romance. The last time she and her sister had spoken, Margot nearly blushed as she listened to Casey's detailed exposition of her love life. It wasn't a problem with their parents; Margo had just spoken with them. She decided that if she hadn't reached Casey by dinnertime, she would call Luke at the sheriff's department.

While Margot was debating her strategies for reaching Casey, Casey was rummaging through her desk, frantically looking for the unmarked disc. She was certain that it had been on her stack of mail when she left for work. She didn't have a cleaning woman (although Luke had hinted a few times that hiring one would be good idea), and she and Luke had left for work together earlier in the day.

"Shit!" Casey slammed the bottom desk drawer and dropped into the desk chair. The only logical explanation, and one that might spell doom for her, was that Luke had stopped home on his lunch break and, clueless about her deception with Judge Clarke, had taken the disc to work to view it or return it to Ben's desk.

Casey had no patience for the office operator. She dialed the emergency number for the sheriff's office and said, somewhat breathlessly, that she needed to speak to Chief Anderson immediately. His voice came on the line before she could compose a credible explanation for her call.

"Luke," she said, now truly breathless, "I've lost the CD—you know, the one I got from Ben's desk. Please tell me you have it. Oh, my god, you have to have it!"

"Calm down, Case. I have it. I've seen it. And frankly, at this point I don't know what the hell all the fuss is about. It's a scan of those half-sheets the judges sign when they've made a ruling in a case. I'll bring it home tonight, and maybe you can make some sense of it. Or should I just take it to Judge Clarke, since she's the one who signed it?"

There was no sound on the line. "Casey—are you still there?"

"Listen, Luke, I'm really sorry I bothered you at work. Bring the disc home, and we'll talk about it. There's some stuff I need to tell you."

Luke heard the click and dial tone before he could respond. "Women! They make such a big deal out of everything."

|48|

BY THE TIME Luke walked through the front door of Casey's apartment, she had a pretty good idea of what was causing all the interest in Ben's disc. If she was right, it might also provide clues as to who wanted Ben Toledo dead. But before they booted up the disc and talked about what it all meant for the court, Casey insisted that Luke listen to what she had done and what she feared it meant for her and for them. She was halfway through her story about her conversation with Judge Clarke and her less than truthful response about the contents of the disc when Luke exploded.

"Are you telling me that you lied? C'mon, Casey, you know better. For chrissakes, you've seen people go to the slammer for that! You've lost your fucking mind, my girl."

Luke was pacing around the small living room and shouting at such a pitch that Casey was sure everyone in the building could hear the noise, even if they couldn't make out the words.

Casey had expected that Luke would be angry. She was already embarrassed and contrite. But the intensity of his outburst had the effect of making her equally angry. "Listen, Luke, my good friend has been murdered, my place of employment has been bombed, my employer is in the hospital, and someone is scaring a judge so much that she's putting pressure on her bailiff for a lousy CD! So why don't you give the righteous outrage thing a rest and see if you can help out here?" By now Casey was in Luke's face, so close she could feel his rapid breath. She backed away and waited.

When she saw him sit down, she let out her own breath and immediately did what she had sworn she would not do. She wept with relief. He wasn't going to leave. The burden of guilt she had carried alone for the last several days was now shared and with someone she trusted.

For his part, Luke simply watched, wondering again why women couldn't just talk these things out over a couple of beers—maybe with a little shouting to let out the steam. But the tears? "Why don't we start with Ben's death and what led us to this fucking disc in the first place?"

It was nearly daylight when they fell asleep, both of them on the couch and both fully dressed. There were a lot of missing pieces to the story Casey told Luke, and they were forced to do some guessing. But in the end, they had a working hypothesis, and they had a list of what each of them could do to help fill in some of the blanks. One thing was certain: whoever wanted the disc had pressured, if not scared, Barbara Clarke, and that person was not likely to give up without a fight.

|49|

THERE IS A powerful sense of anticipation whenever a jury is released to begin its deliberations. That is true in any long case but it's especially in the case in a high-stakes criminal trial. When the prosecution concluded its final closing argument (known to courtroom groupies as the "closing close"), it was time for the judge to instruct the jury. Barbara Clarke tried once again to forge an agreement amongst counsel for a lesser offense to be presented to the jury as an alternative to the first-degree murder charge. Lloyd refused to budge. He was convinced that offering the jury a less onerous choice as a verdict would be like handing the proverbial candy to a baby. "They'll jump all over it, Judge." He turned to face Charlie. "I don't see any way this jury can find first-degree murder. Unless the law changed in Florida while we were trying this case, they need to find my client guilty of this crime beyond a reasonable doubt."

When the judge concluded instructing the jury on their heavy responsibilities, "heavy" was an apt description for a lot of eyelids in the courtroom. The jury charge can take hours in a complex case, but many cases have been successful on appeal to a higher court simply because a judge failed to include something that seemed obvious or repetitive. When Barbara made what she hoped would be her final warning to the jury to refrain from discussing the case with anyone, she smiled at the twelve people seated in the jury box and said, "But I'm happy to remove the prohibition against talking to one another. That is what you must do now, and you must do so with respect for others' opinions and a firm conviction that you will do what is right. That means you will act with integrity and fairness."

Brittany yawned. They had heard all about this during jury orientation. Then they heard it when the judge swore them in for the trial. Now they were hearing it again! She shifted in her chair and yawned again. Her gaze went across the room to Casey. "Let's get it on, honey," she muttered to herself, but loud enough that several people turned and smiled or nodded.

"Getting it on" was the last thing on Casey's mind at that moment. She was outwardly engaged in the business of giving special instructions to the jurors. She knew that they were excited about the deliberations and they were anxious to get started. Casey was anxious too, but only for a break so that she could do some of the things that she and Luke had discussed late into the night. Her first assignment was to go to the Clerk of Criminal Courts and ask if there was a hard copy of the half-sheet they had seen on Ben's disc. If they got lucky, she could make a comparison of the signature on each. As a bailiff, she knew only too well that although most judges had a rubber stamp with their signature embossed on it, they rarely used it, because the local rules of the Appellate Court prohibited any judge from using a stamp for anything other than "housekeeping" matters. A sentencing order in a criminal case was hardly what anyone would consider housekeeping.

Casey was almost finished with the jurors seated in the box and the four alternates who would remain at the courthouse until a verdict was reached when she heard a shout from the back row. "Damnation! I can't do this anymore." Looking up, the source of the shout was obvious, as a large and visibly upset black woman stood and began to make her way out of the jury box. A series of muttered "excuse me" and "pardon me" didn't appease her fellow jurors, who muttered as they shifted in their seats, much like people accommodating a late arrival at a play.

Before the woman could open her mouth, a deputy sheriff known around the courthouse as Amazon Amy took hold of her arm and, without apparent difficulty, turned the upset juror to face her directly. Amazon Amy put her hands on the woman's broad shoulders. "This case has us all riled up. But if you disrupt this process, ma'am, you could be in contempt of court. So I'd advise you to just sit down right here by the railing and wait until you have a chance to talk." The news that the woman would not be returning to her place brought an audible sigh of relief from several jurors in her line of seating.

During the course of the trial, Casey had developed a relationship with a number of the jurors. Mrs. Henderson, the agitated woman now seated outside the jury box, was as dedicated to her task as anyone Casey had ever seen. She was usually the first person to arrive at the jury room in the morning, and she was unfailingly attentive. That was not true of every juror. Alice Shamban was worried about her ill husband and asked for breaks frequently so that she could call and check up on him. Brittany, the young woman from the hair and tanning salon, was openly contemptuous of the whole process. But most of the jurors were respectful and went out of their way to be helpful. Several had appointed themselves in charge of morning donuts and Danish.

Now that Casey had finished her housekeeping instructions, people began to move toward the door to the jury room or toward the exit doors at the back of the courtroom. As Casey walked toward the judge's area, she noticed the large black woman staring at the ceiling but otherwise unmoving. Casey moved quickly.

"Are you all right, Mrs. Henderson?"

The woman moved her eyes from the ceiling to Casey. "I am perfect," she announced in a calm and firm voice. "I can't get this case out of my mind, and the thought that we might sit around here for more of this trial and not be able to do a thing about it—well, it darn near killed me too!" She rose with difficulty from her chair and made her way toward the door to the jury room.

Casey was finally finished with the details of how the jury should proceed to select a foreperson, how to contact the court (meaning her), when they were permitted to take a break, (anytime they wished), and a host of other seemingly mundane items. When she was done, she closed and locked the door to the jury room behind her, setting into motion one of the most fascinating and complex processes in the human drama we call justice.

As she stepped into the general area and saw some of the "regulars" hanging around, she noticed Harold Cohen pacing the floor near the large windows at the end of the hall. His genial smile and wave seemed to have disappeared, and what Casey saw was the face of naked rage. She was shocked, but she was also unprepared for the appearance of the heavyset man who was stepping into the hall from the doorway marked Men's Room. He appeared equally unprepared for their near collision, and her earlier suspicions were now ratcheted so high that she could not simply walk by and ignore him.

The man had already turned away, and Casey had to skip a step to gain ground and catch up to him. "Excuse me." She had raised her voice just a decibel, but it had the effect of jolting him to a standstill. When he turned to face her, she felt her face redden, and she retreated a step.

"You startled me, madam," he said accusingly.

Casey shot back, "No more than your daily presence in our courthouse has startled me, sir. Is there something I can help you with or do you just like our coffee?"

"Aren't you the sassy lass? Sorry, I should have introduced myself weeks ago. I write for one of the British tabloids, and I must say, this dog case has fascinated our readers. You know, of course, that we bred the first of what you people like to call pit bulls. Colorful breed, I daresay, but then we were more interested in wagering on dogfights than using the beasts as weapons. You Americans are so creative." He made an elaborate bow. "Brian Edwards, at your service."

So much for my radar, she thought as she made her way downstairs to the Clerk of Criminal Courts. It wasn't until she approached the long wooden counter to ask for the file containing the material on Ben's disc that she realized she hadn't asked the man why a reporter covering a trial would hang around outside the courtroom instead of sitting inside it.

Upstairs, the heavyset man pushed past a couple of older people carrying lunchboxes that said Amy on the front and sides, boldly penciled along with purple dragons and pink bears. "Move it," the man said brusquely, without even a trace of a foreign accent.

|50|

"MCGINTY, GET THE hell over here!"

Jack didn't even turn his head. He had spent enough nights in the slammer to understand fully the power trips that the guards were on and how gratifying it was to grab a little bit back for yourself. A gentle tap on his left shoulder brought a smile to his face. *So,* he thought as he turned slowly toward the tapper, *I've brought the little fucker to me.* The fist to his face was so swift and well placed that his nose was gushing blood before the smile below it had faded completely. He stepped back into the chest of another guard and knew in an instant that these guys didn't fool around. As a punch to his left kidney pushed him forward, he seesawed into his first assailant and had a final conscious thought about his ancestors in Ireland and the lessons they had learned at the boot of the "unarmed" subjects of Her Majesty. Everyone he knew in South Florida held to the notion that the local cops in the Keys were off-duty fisherman and totally laid back. "Same crap!" he muttered as he went down.

Things had gone badly since Jack roared out of West Palm Beach heading due south on I-95. The combination of being scared, hungry, and hungover gave way rapidly to a craving for alcohol that was uncontrollable. He pulled into a twenty-four-hour Sunoco station and held his breath as he pushed open the door. He spotted the shelves lined with six-packs and headed straight for them, almost drooling when he saw the frosty cooler at the end of the aisle. The door slid heavily to the side, and Jack pulled on the handles of two cardboard containers of his favorite brew . When he hefted them onto the high counter surrounded by a wall of Plexiglas, the clerk nodded briefly and said, "ID or passport, Mac."

Jack reached into his jacket, realizing that he had nothing. No wallet, no cash, nothing.

"Shit, man, I left it in the car." As he turned, he stuffed two bottles into his jacket pockets and walked toward the door.

This wasn't the first time that a Plexiglas security barrier stopped the good guys from catching a thief. The clerk, a middle-aged guy sporting a sagging belly and a two-tone beard, wasn't nearly fast enough to stop Jack. But there was nothing slow about his eyes, and he nailed the plate before the car was out of the lot.

By the time Jack had passed Islamorada, he had acquired a passport and a wallet from a nice young couple shopping for an engagement ring in a flea market at Sample Road. But his best efforts to ditch the car, or at least the plate, had failed, and as he approached Marathon, he found himself leading a caravan of police cars. The two guys who approached the driver's side of his car with rifles raised looked anything but friendly.

It took several days for Jack to arrange bail through his sister, Marie, who always said "Never again" but never meant it. He knew he'd taken advantage of her, but he always figured that since she had him pegged for a deadbeat, he didn't want to disappoint her.

Now, as he headed north toward West Palm, he ached all over, and he knew he would go on a bender as soon as he got close enough to home to hit up some old friends in Lake Worth. He was beat up, he was scared, he was confused, and he was just plain tired. A bad package for a man with a long list of earned enemies

|51|

MAGGIE CAINE HAD worked for the West Palm Beach Clerk of Courts since her junior year in high school. She'd been a quiet kid then, and most people took no notice of her. But she was a definite presence now, some thirty years later, and no one liked her. She was bossy, mean-spirited, and uncooperative with everyone but the male judges. "Don't mess with Maggie" was a courthouse mantra, one that Maggie relished and actively encouraged. She proved true to her reputation when Casey appeared at her desk.

"Listen, girlie, we don't hand out original court documents to anybody, not even a bailiff, without permission from the judge or the presiding judge. So you get me something in writing, and I'll get you what you want." True to her reputation, Maggie never looked up from the pile of papers on her desk as she delivered her answer to Casey's request. Casey stood rooted to the spot, feeling like a child who has just been dismissed by a teacher. She was fighting the temptation to unleash a recital of some of her best profanity, when she spotted Barbara Clarke across the rows of desks. The judge was coming directly toward her and, it seemed to Casey, with an angry look on her face.

"I just spoke with Luke. You're fired, Casey." Barbara turned on her heel and headed toward the door. No one who witnessed the scene needed inside information to know that something dramatic had just happened and that it wasn't good news for Casey.

Maggie, however, had heard every word. She looked up from her seat at Casey's deeply flushed face and smirked. "I guess you won't be needing those papers after all."

Casey didn't waste a minute. She raced through the swinging door of the clerk's office, nearly knocking over the cart of files being pushed along like a newborn. "Judge. Judge Clarke, please wait just a minute." Barbara Clarke stopped in her tracks but didn't turn to face Casey. She waited until Casey was beside her before turning and looking into Casey's face with a look of sheer fury.

"I know you have been under tremendous pressure, Casey, and I've tried to rationalize your conduct six ways to Sunday, all to no avail. You deliberately misled me about the disc that you removed from Ben's desk and before you try to give me an excuse for your behavior, let me be clear— there is no excuse. Firing you is my only recourse other than seeking an indictment for obstruction of justice."

|52|

JURY ROOMS IN newly built courthouses tend to look uncannily similar to their antique counterparts, and anyone who has the misfortune of spending a lot of time in one will find themselves looking for Henry Fonda to appear at any moment. In fact, the biggest difference between the room in *Twelve Angry Men* and the room now occupied by the Diemert jury was the absence of windows. As a result, no matter how high the fans or how low the air conditioning, the room felt stifling.

As instructed by Casey, the jurors had seated themselves around the table in accordance with their number. There was an awkward silence when everyone was seated. Twelve pairs of eyes scanned the room, wondering who would be the first to speak. More than one person did a flash survey of the sex, race, and age ratios of the group, and everyone noticed that women outnumbered the men by two to one.

"Okay, everybody, um . . . the bailiff, um . . . told us the first thing to do was, um . . . to choose a chairman." Clive Barstow was a retired farmer. He had a round face topped by a gray crew cut. His easy smile and equally easy personality made him popular among the jurors. "Um, I don't mean any offense, ladies. I'm just used to, um, chairman, y'know."

The silence that followed Clive's remarks was awkward.

"Say, Mr. Barstow, how about you be the chairman? Unless someone else be wanting it, a course." Mrs. Henderson shifted in the well-padded swivel chair to survey the other jurors.

A handsome man who looked too young to be retired, raised his hand. "I second Miss Henderson's motion." Several other jurors nodded in agreement, and someone at the end of the table said loudly, "Call for the vote." A few jurors listlessly raised a hand, and without any dissent, there was general agreement and a smattering of applause at the table. No one, including Clive, was quite sure what the next step was, so Clive made his first executive decision and called for a restroom break.

Brittany, who was seated next to Mrs. Henderson, went immediately into the corner and onto her Blackberry. She sent an urgent, terribly misspelled, and almost incoherent text to her favorite uncle. She wanted to warn him to get out of West Palm Beach. "Ioverherd this woman say they were looking for yur sentents sheets. Dont no y."

Brittany's fantasy career in sleuthing had taken an unexpected turn while she lingered during a recess in the ground floor women's room. She was concentrating on the application of her new lip gloss when her attention was drawn to the two women near the sink at the end of the room. The conversation between someone named Maggie and a bookish-looking woman carefully washing every finger on her hands was about a bailiff Maggie had recently "put in her place." Brittany had not paid attention, since her bangs were of much greater interest to her than these two old biddies and their stupid victories. That was until she heard her name.

"McGinty. He was one of Clarke's cases. Damned if I know what Kanterman's bailiff wanted, but a lot of people seem heated up about this case—even the judge." The speaker was now leaning against the wall, and she caught Brittany's eye just as she turned in their direction. Brittany ignored the woman's raised eyebrow and returned her gaze to the mirror. The older women clattered on their heels across the marble floor and out the swinging door.

Balancing her latte, Louis Vuitton knockoff, and *Tanning for Tots* magazine, Brittany decided it was probably just a coincidence. But she was definitely going to send a text to Uncle Jack as soon as she had an opportunity.

The opportunity to send the garbled text came soon enough. Not so the opportunity for it to be read, since Jack's cell phone was long dead and gone.

Any day now, if things didn't look up for him, the same might be said of Jack.

|53|

BY THE TIME Casey got to her office, the pain in her chest was excruciating. She was in good physical shape, but not good enough for this kind of stress. Stunned to the point of clinical shock, she had not shed a tear but stood, red-faced and panting, her eyes fixed on the calendar that hung on the wall behind her desk. Next to the calendar, leaning on the tall, gray steel file cabinet was someone she dreaded seeing but wanted nearby more than anyone else.

Neither one of them moved or spoke. Casey's gaze moved to the window and held there, for all the world fixed on some fascinating scene unfolding in empty space.

"Casey. I'm so sorry. It was unavoidable. Lives were hanging in the balance, including yours." Luke's voice was raspy. His words were released from his lips on ragged, abbreviated breaths. His eyes never left Casey's face. Hers never left the empty sky outside the window.

It was absurd, she knew, but as she stood there, paralyzed with rage and confusion, all she could think of was how perfect the sky seemed, a robin's-egg blue that blessed the city only in late summer, as though to tease people with what would soon be only a memory as the rainy season began.

"Excuse me, Miss Casey, but I've been ringing that buzzer for a while now. These folks need a break, and . . ." Clive's voice trailed off as he took in the scene. "Well, I guess we can wait just a few more minutes." He was backing our of the room when Casey whirled on him and said in tense, high-pitched voice, "Maybe Chief Anderson can help you out, Mr. Barstow. All the bailiffs on this floor seem to have been disposed of—by death or betrayal." Casey grabbed her purse from the drawer of her desk and charged out the door. She didn't give a damn about the jury or whether they all peed in their pants.

Despite Luke's limited experience with women and especially with one as strong-willed as Casey, he knew better than to follow her. Besides, it was better that she was out of the courthouse and might therefore be out of harm's way. Still, he knew she'd be a target, and not just because of the disc. There were now four people who had knowledge of the fraudulent sentence of probation for Jack McGinty, but only he knew the piece of the case that was the tie to Ben's murder and the threats to Judge Clarke and to Casey.

Luke got hold of Amazon Annie, and the jury was soon attended to and back at work. As he headed out of the courthouse, Luke mused that in a romantic melodrama, he would be rushing to Casey's side, filled with remorse. Instead, he was filled with anxiety. Too many people were dead, and more might be if he couldn't connect the dots—the new favorite cliché in law enforcement.

He considered, but only briefly, asking for backup as he climbed into the driver's seat of his jeep. But since he expected to find no one and probably nothing of great value at Jack McGinty's house, it didn't really seem necessary.

He was right. That's because he missed McGinty by a heartbeat.

|54|

WHILE CASEY WAS wandering around the ground floor of the building, and while Luke was looking into windows and cursing himself for not getting a search warrant for McGinty's house, Judge Clarke was revisiting the McGinty case and asking herself how a nice guy like Ben Toledo ever got mixed up in this mess. She was already certain of one thing, one very disturbing thing. Her husband was involved.

When Luke had walked into her chambers that morning, she was shocked by his appearance and concerned about his conduct. Luke Anderson was not the sort of man to appear without an appointment or, at the very least, a polite knock on the door. Still, it was common knowledge at the courthouse that he and Casey were an item, and her first assumption was that his visit had to do with that relationship.

Ten minutes later, the judge was pacing the oriental rug in front of her large mahogany desk. "Wait a minute, Luke. This makes no sense to me. Why would Casey deliberately lie to me? What possible motive could she have?"

Luke had remained close to the door throughout his recitation of what he knew about the disc, about Ben, and about Jack McGinty.

"First of all, I'm not here to explain or defend Casey's choice. She acted under pressure, including the sure knowledge that something was terribly amiss here and that you might be in grave danger. And I don't think she's wrong on either point. We know that your former bailiff, Ben, forged your signature on a half-sheet granting probation to a man convicted of killing a small child while driving drunk. Pretty big, bad stuff right there.

"We also know that some guy posing as a foreign reporter has been sneaking around, including a pattern of regular surveillance of your chambers area.

"Finally, we know that you yourself expressed serious concerns about obtaining Ben's disc. What we don't know is why you're concerned and whether you are being threatened or blackmailed."

Judge Clarke sat down in the small chair usually occupied by supplicants asking for a light sentence for a client or for a quick decision on a probation violation. The tall black woman looked diminutive, hunched over and staring at the rug.

"It's a good thing you're not here to advocate for Casey. What she did is unforgiveable. It was disloyal and deceptive, and I'm not sure how to deal with it, other than to dismiss her immediately." She looked up long enough to see Luke wince and take a step back toward the wall, as if for support.

"As far as my concerns, they are just that. Mine. So unless you have a subpoena, I'd suggest we end this conversation."

The awkward silence lasted for several minutes. Barbara had turned away so that she didn't have to look at Luke's face, anguished and so openly vulnerable.

"I didn't come here, Judge, to get the woman I love fired from her job. I came because I sense a rolling stone, a crisis building around these issues, and I don't know enough yet to get it under control and put a stop to it. You know things I don't know. But I do know that as long as you act as an enabler for whoever you are protecting, your life and some other lives are in grave danger."

Without waiting for a reply, Luke left the room. The judge was still hunched over in her chair, staring at the rug and looking for answers. Her addiction to Ellis was beginning to have consequences far beyond her own happiness, or lack of it. It now threatened the safety of her colleagues and the integrity of the very system she was sworn to uphold. She got no answers from the rug, and she knew that she would do no better with Ellis. Without hard evidence of foul play by Ellis, she couldn't go to anyone with an unsubstantiated accusation. She could only hope that the truth would be revealed before someone else got hurt.

As she stood to return to her desk while she waited for the jury's verdict, she felt a distinct chill of apprehension—the enemy of hope.

|55|

THE JURY ROOM table was a mess. Exhibits and transcripts were piled in the center of the table. Most of the exhibits were encased in large plastic bags, and jurors had been supplied with clear gloves to wear should they choose to remove the exhibits and handle them. Several criminal law journals had reported cases of hepatitis that were traced to blood residue on items handled by employees or jurors in other cases, so the gloves became a necessity, just like pencils and legal pads. Most of the jurors had their personal belongings on the table as well, and the scene gave the impression of people hard at work and overcome by chaos.

Unfortunately, the greatest source of chaos was the

stymied effort to reach a verdict. Clive had tried unsuccessfully to proceed in an orderly fashion, reviewing the elements of the crime, reviewing the evidence, reviewing the testimony by witnesses and experts. After nearly six hours, every aspect of the trial seemed to have been accorded equal weight in their deliberations. There was not much disagreement on what had happened or which witnesses had been credible and which seemed like liars or just people looking for their fifteen minutes of fame.

Clive was flustered. The judge's instructions had been clear: do not take a test vote immediately. Review all the evidence carefully, and discuss it with a view toward allowing everyone to speak. Do remember that the burden you carry is heavy and will affect a number of people, most certainly the life of the defendant, but the lives of others as well. Do not allow any one piece of evidence or one person's testimony to outweigh everything else you have seen and heard.

So far he'd done a pretty good job, but it was getting late, and the youngest member of the jury, a college senior named Gary, became quite agitated about holding over for another day. Clive was at a loss.

As usual, Mrs. Henderson came to his rescue. She was standing against the wall, finding that place far more comfortable than squeezing into the captain's-style chair at the table. "Hey, hey, hey." She looked down the room to Clive. "You all may have this fantasy that you gonna decide this thing today. Not me. No, sir, not me. I spent all this time squashed into those tiny seats out there, and I ain't rushing to judge this thing out."

"I think that's called *rushing to judgment*," muttered the female juror seated next to Clive. She received a number of dirty looks for her interruption.

"Honey, I don't care what you call it. This here's my job, and I'm gonna do it right, y'hear?"

Everyone began speaking at once, and Maggie, who had

been recruited from the clerk's office to stand in as the bailiff for Judge Clarke, was rapping loudly on the locked door.

Clive, who found Casey both pleasant and attractive, had exactly the opposite reaction to Maggie. "Sorry about the noise," he said, holding the door open with his foot. "I think we're going to break for the night and come back in the morning." Over Maggie's shoulder he caught a glimpse of the older man who had been seated at the back of the courtroom every day of the trial. Clive had been told by other jurors that the man was the victim's father.

Gee, Clive thought to himself, *it's kind of surprising that they let the guy back here.* Clive saw himself as a rough-and-ready guy, the sort who wasn't nervous or queasy at the horror movies that his wife and daughters freaked out over. But just then he felt a premonition of something bad, really bad.

He turned away from Harold Cohen and tried to physically shake off the feeling. He succeeded, and walking back to the table, he felt confident that the worst that might happen to any of them was a lousy meal and a bad bed while they were sequestered for the night.

Standing in the hallway near the jury room, Harold Cohen nearly wept with relief. He knew he was not allowed in this area. Worse, had anyone made a fuss, or had a deputy sheriff patted him down, the gun that was now "sequestered" in his left front pants pocket would have been taken, and he would have been removed from the building or worse. Trying to regain his composure, Harold made his way back to the law library, where the same young man he had met the day before lingered over his computer. Since it was well before closing time, Harold dispensed with the small talk and went directly to "his" bookshelf. He stored the weapon and left the library.

The young librarian looked at the older man, curious that his visit had been so brief and uneventful. "What the hell? These old folks probably don't even remember what they came for in the first place." Turning back to his Facebook page, he debated putting the picture of himself at a party when he was totally wasted onto his homepage. This time his intuition was working well, and he deleted the picture.

When he saw the story about Harold Cohen on CNN a few days later, and learned where and how the gun had been secreted in such a perfect hiding place, he'd realize what a chance he and his intuition had missed—a chance to be a real hero.

|56|

IF ANYONE HAD told Jack McGinty that he would someday want to get to an AA meeting, he'd have split a gut laughing. But here he was, flat on his back on the rear seat of his car, watching his whole body shake from alcohol withdrawal, and all he could think of was the promises on page 83 of the Big Book. It occurred to him that if could get to a meeting, somebody might help him get a pill to calm him down, might even offer him a place to stay. He held his hands in front of his face, watching them twitch and flutter like a pair of ballerinas. He tried to sit up, but his body was stiff from lying wedged between the back doors of the small car. He finally maneuvered out of the vise by putting his left leg in the air and throwing his body across the seat.

"Holy mother of God! Who built these fucking things, anyways?" It took a full half an hour to straighten up and stretch enough to face the thought of crawling back in the car. Jack had decided that his better course of action, now that he was out of his predicament, was to put off the "cure" for another day and instead pay a visit to his partner, Ellis, the guy who had made this mess and who happened to owe him a nice pile of money—money that might buy him a berth on a trawler headed to the Abacos. The more Jack thought about it, the more he calculated he was owed—a pretty tidy sum when you added being an accessory to murder on top of his cut of the drug sales.

It was after midnight when Jack pulled up to the Ellises' house. It was a large home in a trendy area of West Palm Beach, built in the post-Depression, prewar stucco favored by people of all classes. Some would describe it as a mansion, but it was just a big house and a proper place for a circuit court judge to live.

The house was dark. Not a single light burned on any of the three floors that Jack could make out with the help of the streetlight. He'd never been here before, never even been near the place, and Ellis has always made it clear that he was never to call him at his home or be anywhere near it. But Jack was out of options.

When he opened the car door, he froze. Loud barking pierced the quiet, and he could hear the hulk of a large dog slamming against a chain-link fence. No lights appeared in the house behind him or in Ellis's house, so he closed the door to just before it latched and raced across the narrow street.

His hands were shaking so badly that he had to use one to support the other so he could knock on the window that was next to the large wooden door. Nothing. No lights appeared, and there was no sound of anyone approaching. He squinted through the tiny mullioned glass partition, but he couldn't make out a thing. He leaned against the massive door, thankful that at least the dog had shut up.

"You stupid prick!" The arm that coiled around his neck was massive, and Jack instinctively reached up to pull it away. Instead, he found himself dragged down the brick steps and into the well-manicured, stately bushes that surrounded the house. Snot was running from his nose, and he felt his eyes enlarging as though they were going to pop out of his head. Jack fought hard. He twisted his hand so he could latch onto Ellis's belt, but it was an almost comical effort. Ellis simply lifted him, like a stuffed animal, into the air and threw him down onto the carefully pruned edge of the flowerbeds. Only one person was breathing hard now, and that was the attacker. The other one, the life of the party, was dead.

|57|

CASEY HAD HEARD the expression "clean out your desk" in the movies, but it seemed too corny to describe what she was doing at the moment. While Maggie stood guard at the entryway to Judge Kanterman's chambers, Casey filled a banker's box with pictures of her parents and sister, Margot, along with the paperbacks she had meant to read if she ever got the chance. She opened the large bottom file drawer, and Maggie moved quickly into hovering position, but there were no files, only a pair of well-worn sneakers and an old lunch bag that gave off the faint aroma of a banana peel.

Cleaning out her desk was easy for Casey compared with cleaning Luke's presence out of her life and her apartment, in precisely that order. She refused every attempt Luke made to connect with her. He had called several times, each time leaving a message of apology and suggesting that they meet to discuss what had happened. She had not returned the calls, but she had spent hours on the phone with Margot. It was impossible to explain to her sister, or anyone else, the confusion she felt. Outing her to Judge Clarke without a warning was unforgiveable. So was the judge firing her in a public place.

But the mental gymnastics were too much for her, and at her mother's suggestion, seconded by Margot, she packed Luke's few personal possessions in a large, black trash bag and placed them outside the apartment manager's door. At her request, the manager had phoned Luke at the sheriff's office to ask that he remove the bag as soon as possible.

She had now filled a similar bag of trash from her desk. While Maggie stood guard, Casey quickly looked around the area for anything she might have left behind. Something moved just outside her line of vision, and as she looked toward the glass partition that separated the antechamber and elevator area, she caught a glimpse of someone who had quickly materialized and was just as quickly gone. She wasted no time and began to move quickly toward the door.

"Excuse me, but if you're done, you're done. Know what I mean?" Maggie closed the pencil drawer with her ample hip and glared at Casey. "I've got a job to do. Yours!"

By this time Casey was out the door and past the partition, heading toward the hall that led to the jury room and the back stairway. She stopped at the hall's end and was amazed when she saw nothing. The heavy door, which for fire safety purposes could be opened easily, led to a stairwell from which the only exit was at the parking garage floor, immediately in front of the guard's desk. If anyone had been hanging around outside her office and had used the stairs to flee the building, he would not go undetected.

Casey had a pretty good idea who the phantom was, and she felt the same unease she had felt around him before. *If he's a reporter from England, I'm a cosmonaut from Russia.*

The stairs were concrete with steel strips on the edges. A midway landing at the flight to the ground floor exit left only a half dozen steps to the large door with the push plate in the center. Casey made no effort to conceal her descent, as her heels made a loud clanging sound on each step. It didn't matter. The man in question was standing at the bottom, waiting patiently for her.

|58|

LUKE WAS DRIVING like a maniac. Every car light he could pulse or flash was going full tilt, and so was his siren. Even though the traffic between the hospital and the Courthouse was light, the distance was substantial, and Luke briefly considered calling for help. God knew there was plenty available. But his conversation with Janet Kanterman had persuaded him that calling in the infantry wouldn't matter here. If he was right about who was the danger and how much of a danger he was to everyone's safety, then Luke had to trap him where he could neutralize him.

He and Judge Kanterman had talked at length about the bombing investigation, with Luke admitting that his department and the specialists from the ATF office in Miami were at a dead end. They hadn't found any connection between the dog case and the bailiff's murder, and the only activity that had seemed to gel into what you could call a lead to hard evidence was the focus on Ben's copy of the half-sheet in a case that was closed weeks ago. As he spoke, he was aware that the judge seemed greatly improved, but Luke was conscious of her fragility, and it took a while to fill Janet in on the mess created by Casey taking the disc and then lying to Judge Clarke about its contents.

"Dear God. I can't believe that Ben would get involved with anything like this. It's ridiculous and not at all like the young man I knew." Janet's eyes had widened, and she was waving her hand as if to make it all disappear from her mind's view. She recounted her interactions with Ben in the days immediately before the nightmare unfolded in the garage. Her memory of the events on that night was blessedly blurred, but she was certain that one of the people who ran from behind her car was very tall. He actually seemed vaguely familiar to her, but her efforts to force her mind to recall his face only resulted in great stress and the kind of blood pressure spikes that her surgeons were determined to avoid. But it was not her blood pressure that was out of control at the moment. It was her guest.

Luke's small wooden chair fell on its side as he stood abruptly. He tripped over the legs of her tray table and, barely regaining his balance, raced out the door.

Despite the sirens and flashers, Luke drove carefully. He had heard too many horror stories about injuries and even deaths from ambulances or police cars blasting through busy intersections, the officers always assuming that the other drivers heard or saw them. The only thing he could ignore and did on his race toward the courthouse was his concern about Casey. At least, he thought to himself, she had no reason to be around the courthouse anymore, and that would put her outside the zone of danger.

|59|

BRITTANY WAS SOBBING like a baby. She had plenty of company. Most of the women jurors, and at least one man, were teary-eyed. Mrs. Henderson was swaying back and forth like a preacher in ecstasy, and even Clive Barstow, who had managed to keep his cool for the last two days, was loudly blowing his outsize nose into a rumpled hand-kerchief.

Each of the jurors had signed the verdict form. There was no hung jury here. They were close to a verdict from the get-go, and but for two stubborn holdouts, they would have been done in less than the day and a half it had taken. They had sent only one question to the judge:

Dear Judge,
If a person is so drunk that they don't know what they're doing, is everything they do still intentional?
Yours truly,
Clive (the jury foreman)

Barbara Clarke had called the lawyers at their offices or on their mobiles and asked them to return to the court to discuss the answer. It wasn't as if she didn't know the answer, but the rules required that she read the question to the attorneys, allow them to comment, and then direct that the bailiff write her answer on the same sheet of paper as the question was written. The sheet would become a permanent part of the case file and available on appeal. In response to the call, Lloyd sent a young associate, since Lloyd was tied up answering questions from the sheriff's office and the ATF team about his former client, Jack McGinty. Charlie Graham likewise sent an underling, as he was still licking his wounds about blurting out the news of Amy Cohen's illegitimate child.

It didn't matter much who attended, because the answer was as old as the English law on which most American laws are based. Although insanity and, in some states, "diminished capacity" might be a defense for an intentional crime, imbibing alcohol or drugs is, in and of itself, an intentional act, and a person is responsible for his or her actions that flow from that choice.

The judge's answer was short and to the point:

Dear Mr. Barstow,
The answer to the jury's question is yes.
Judge Barbara Clarke

Clive dutifully reread both the question and answer. A juror who had said very little during the deliberations thus far exclaimed, "That's it for me. Let's vote again." The judge's answer apparently affected the other holdout too, because this time the verdict was unanimous.

Clive rang the buzzer for Maggie, who knocked, unlocked the door, and then poked her scowling face around the doorframe. "If you folks are planning on lunch today, and if you expect me to get it for you, you better get a move on."

Instead of an answer, Clive handed her the envelope into which he had placed the verdict form.

"You're done?" Maggie asked as she snatched the envelope from Clive's hand without even waiting for an answer. "Let me see if I can get everybody here, and then you can get your own damn lunches." Without catching her breath, she pulled the door shut and shot down the hall to her temporary desk. She knew Judge Clarke was in her chambers, and surely the State Attorney's office had someone they could send. Lloyd was the only problem, but she had a bunch of numbers for him, and she began dialing them, all the while praying for success. She hated this bailiff job and longed to return to her post as chief clerk and contrarian.

|60|

COURT REPORTERS ARE usually the first to know when something important has happened in a case that's gone to the jury. Once the call came to the reporters' workroom to send someone up to Judge Clarke's floor, word of a probable verdict spread quickly through the Justice Complex, and the benches inside the courtroom began to fill up with court personnel, witnesses in other cases, and people waiting to pay tickets or see a public defender. Harold Cohen had no interest in taking one of those seats. He had his position carefully staked out just outside the courtroom doors. He was traveling light. Other than the discreet bulge in his pocket, he had nothing on his person: no wallet, no papers of any kind that would identify him before his letter reached Miriam in Bloomfield Hills. She had cried and begged when he ordered her to stay away from West Palm Beach when the verdict was announced. But his resolve was unshakeable. If the system forced him to exact his own punishment for Amy's brutal death, he would take his own life, along with that of the killer. It was one thing for Miriam to mourn for him—that had become a way of life for her. It was another to stand by while he was tried for murder and—worst possible outcome—, sentenced to life in prison, where he would literally be a ball and chain that she dragged for the rest of her life.

The atmosphere on the fourth floor was almost festive, as people gossiped about the twists and turns of the case and all of the surprises, not the least of which was Judge Clarke firing her bailiff. "If this keeps up, Clarke will need her own pool of substitute bailiffs. She's shedding them like snakeskin." The clerks and secretaries from other courts were gathered near the elevators, chatting animatedly while they moved their gazes over the phalanx of young assistant prosecutors who had come to celebrate what they assumed would be an easy win for the state.

Inside the courtroom, Lloyd Schwartzman was conferring with his client. Josiah's appearance was startling. He'd shaved his head, including his eyebrows. He wore a pair of rumpled blue jeans, a torn white T-shirt, and unlaced sneakers. Perhaps even more surprising, he was clear-eyed and absolutely sober.

Lloyd was no more fond of his client today than he had been on the first day they met. But over the course of the trial he'd developed a kind of pity for the guy. Lloyd had been sober for most of his adult life, and he credited AA for saving him from what was beginning to look like the classic slide of a junkie and a drunk headed straight for death or for death row. It was the unexpected intervention of his stepfather that he also credited for the miracle. Big

Al Stark married Sydelle Schwartzman not long after her husband was killed in Vietnam. Even though everyone in Sydelle's family knew that Lloyd had a problem, acknowledging drunks and druggies was not a thing people did in the Jewish community. But Big Al, a husky brick-and-mortar contractor, came from a family that talked about little else, and it took less than one week around his new stepson to tell him everything he needed to know. Lloyd's mother believed to this day that her son had voluntarily checked into a rehab center in Minnesota. That's because she never saw the black eye that he sported as a souvenir of his encounter with Big Al, a preview of the beating that was guaranteed if Lloyd refused Al's generous offer of help.

Josiah Diemert had not been so lucky. And it was apparent that he was dressed for today's jury verdict, one he obviously expected to doom him to life in a Florida prison. Someone had prepared him for the fact that if the jury issued a guilty verdict, he would be taken immediately into custody. *Ergo,* thought Lloyd, *dress-down day for the defendant.*

In fact, everyone seated at the attorney tables was ready to have this ordeal end. A murder trial in a small town was unusual enough. But add to that another murder, a very ill judge, and a bombing at the courthouse, and this bit of jurisprudence was already poised for some hall of fame.

Josiah looked around the courtroom. Everything about what could be loosely called his life since Amy died was still a blur. Oh, he understood the legalities all right, but he didn't understand what the rest of the crap was about. The dude who got killed in the parking garage had nothing to do with him and Amy, or with Butch, for that matter. And the first judge on the case, who everybody on his so-called legal team kept telling him was his best shot at acquittal, pops a fucking aneurysm, and the capper is that he doesn't even know what the fuck happened that night. He's gonna spend the rest of his life rotting in some stinking prison for something he doesn't remember.

The door to the judge's area opened, and the mean-faced bitch who'd replaced the tall, nice-looking bailiff shouted above the noisy chatter. "Okay, listen up people. The judge is in a meeting so it's going to be a few more minutes. If you leave the courtroom, so does your ticket to this circus."

"Now what?" Josiah turned to Lloyd and was annoyed to see that he was paying no attention to him.

Lloyd had bigger problems than waiting for this verdict. He had seen the infamous half-sheet giving Jack McGinty probation for a drunken hit-and-run that killed a little girl. Jesus! It still made no sense to him. Why would Ben get involved with a lowlife like his former client? And where the hell *was* his former client?

One thing was certain. Lloyd was going to have to do some heavy lifting with the bar association to explain away his ethical lapse in dumping McGinty on the public defender without a judge's consent.

"Anybody home?" Josiah barked in Lloyd's ear. Lloyd decided he liked this guy better when he was stoned out of his mind.

"Asshole." Lloyd replied with an open sneer and disappeared through door toward the bailiff's desk. If Casey was still hanging around, maybe she could give him a head's-up on all this crap coming down.

Casey was hanging around, all right, but she was getting a head's-up of her own.

|61|

ELLIS WAS STRETCHED out on the couch in his wife's chambers. His feet hung over the arm, and he looked uncomfortable to Barbara.

"So what exactly do you want to me do, Ellis? I can't give you a pass on drug dealing like Ben gave to your buddy Jack. And I sure as hell don't want to hear your story again about how Jack accidently killed Ben. You were there. Nothing else matters. Don't you get it?"

"I'll tell you what I don't get. I don't get how you think you're gonna drop the dime on me. Last I heard, there's this thing called spousal immunity and while you might not like it so much these days, I am your spouse. " Ellis swung his long legs to the floor and sat up in one elegant motion. "There were four people who could hook me into this mess. Now it's down to just one."

Barbara had stood near the window up until this moment. She now crossed the room slowly until she was directly in front of Ellis. "Stand up, Ellis." She paused and took a step back as he rose to his full height. "And get the hell out of my office and out of my life." She turned back toward her desk. "Oh, and by the way, there is no spousal immunity when there is a threat of imminent harm to a third party. Now go!"

Maggie, who was diligently staring at the phone and mentally ordering it to ring and signal the beginning of court, considered herself an expert in a myriad of different things, including guns. After all, she dealt with them all day as a clerk: orders for evidence production, copies of indictments for carrying concealed weapons, guns used in robberies, guns used to murder. But before this moment, she'd never actually heard the sound of a gun being fired. Her mouth was wide open, just forming the "What?" when big arms shoved her aside. As she fell back into the chair, Amazon Annie was pounding on the door to Judge Clarke's chambers.

"Mayday, mayday! Backup! Clarke." Annie was shouting into the tiny microphone clipped to her shirt collar. "Repeat. Mayday, mayday, shooter here!"

Several deputy sheriffs pushed through the small crowd that had come out of the courtroom to find the source of the commotion. One of the deputies began to urge the crowd away from the area. "Let's move it, folks. Nothing here. You can just go back into the courtroom. There you go. Let's keep it moving."

The door opened. Blood was running down the side of Judge Clarke's head. As she stepped forward, Ellis came into view. His hand was grasping his wife's arm so tightly that it wound once around completely. Annie took a step forward.

"I wouldn't do that, ma'am." His voice was calm, but the hand that raised the gun was shaking visibly. The crowd that had formed needed no further encouragement to back away. People were running and screaming as they fought to get out of Ellis's sight.

"Ellis. Drop the weapon. Do it now!"

Ellis looked toward Luke. "The last time I heard those words, man, I shot the lady who said them." He waved the gun toward Barbara. "So here is how it's going down. My lovely bride and I are going to take a little trip together. You folks, on the other hand, are going into the courtroom, and you're going to stay there." His gaze took in the deputy sheriffs and Luke. "If you even peek out those doors, your dear Judge Clarke is going to be very dead." The area was empty except for an older guy in a suit and tie. "Shoo!" he barked at the guy.

Ellis advanced toward the group as they backed into the courtroom. Still holding Barbara with one hand, he jabbed the elevator button with the other.

Harold Cohen suddenly put it all together. No judge—no jury—no verdict—no punishment! "Oh, no, you don't!" he yelled.

Ellis turned. The first shot smashed into his abdomen. The second went wild and struck the elevator. And then it was quiet. Except for the sobbing of the man dressed impeccably for what he had planned would be the day of reckoning for Josiah Diemert.

Harold dropped the gun. "God, have mercy. Please have mercy on me. Please have mercy." He continued to sob, choking out his mantra as Luke and Annie brought him into the courtroom. The elevator door had closed before the shot that killed Ellis was fired. Barbara stumbled out of the elevator on the first floor and into the arms of one of a dozen guards who had been told to secure the perimeter and be armed and ready while the crisis unfolded. Their radios came alive in a concert of static and shouted orders.

Luke confirmed that Ellis was dead. He did not consult with anyone about his decision to take Harold into protective custody. The man had saved Barbara Clarke's life, and perhaps the lives of others, but he'd also killed a man, and he couldn't just walk away. At a minimum, they would need to know why he was carrying a gun and how he got it into the courthouse.

"Oh, my god! The jury!" Maggie, who had disappeared at the first opportunity, stood in the midst of scores of police officers and shrieked. She scrambled for the key ring she'd dropped hurriedly on her desk when she departed and raced down the hall.

Clive looked up when the door opened. Several jurors were still napping.

Brittany angrily tapped her nail file on the table. "For heaven's sake, with all that racket out there, you'd think the trial was finished without us."

While Maggie tried to explain the horrific events of the last half hour, Luke noticed a large banker's box and a black trash bag sitting next to the door. Casey's oversized purse was on the desk.

He tapped Maggie on the shoulder. She gave him her most annoyed look.

"Is this Casey's?" He pointed to the purse. "Where is she, Maggie? Why would she leave this sitting here? Any idea where she went?"

"Whoa, big boy. One at a time. Yes, it's Casey's, and I don't know where she went, except she ran off toward the exit after she saw some guy near our . . ." Maggie didn't finish. There was no point. Her audience was gone.

He saw her the minute he hit the street. She was sitting on a low brick wall across the street from the garage entrance. She looked terrible. Her hair was disheveled, and her shirt was twisted around her waist like someone trying to undress with one hand. She had shielded her eyes from the late afternoon sun as she watched people milling around the entrances to the courthouse. Luke crossed the street and approached her cautiously.

Casey looked up and said nothing. Luke sat down on the wall beside her and reached over for her hand. To his great relief, she didn't pull away.

Finally, she spoke, though not turning her head in his direction. "How did you figure it out? We both knew about the McGinty mess, and I'm the one who found the small caches of pills all over the area where Ben worked. But that only connected Ben and McGinty, who I figured had probably killed Ben and was putting pressure on Barbara Clarke to get back the only incriminating evidence." Casey turned toward Luke and gave him a grin that lit up the street like the noonday sun. "C'mon, Luke, I've been trying to piece it together since I almost killed myself, or got killed, chasing this guy down the staircase."

Luke let out a sigh. "Let's start with McGinty. He was in no place to put pressure on a judge. C'mon! The guy's a convicted felon. So it had to be somebody else, somebody who was at risk because of the connection between McGinty and the judge." He was pleased to note that he had Casey's full attention now. "That could be several people. Lloyd was one, of course. He was McGinty's lawyer when the phony sentence was issued, and he was in a position to blame it on both Ben and the judge. But Lloyd's profile didn't fit anything we designed as a pattern or a person of interest."

Luke stopped here and reached for the hand that had slipped out of his while he was talking. "You're not going to like this, Case. And I'm telling you I fought it as best I could, but . . ."

"Fuck!" Casey was on her feet. "I was a suspect, right?"

Her arms were akimbo and people nearby had turned to stare. "I can't believe this. It makes no sense. I'm the one who found the disc and told you about it right away. And what's my motive, Mister Genius? What did you and the big boys from Miami figure I had to get out of this?" She turned away, and Luke thought she was about to storm off and leave him sitting there. She didn't. She sat down beside him and, regaining her composure with difficulty, told him to go on with his "inane analysis."

Luke didn't even try for her hand this time. "So, we have a bombing that seems tied to nothing, a murder that's connected to a lowlife drunk, and a disc that suggests that someone is messing with the system, but for no motive we can find." He turned to Casey. "In the end, it was a man's sneaker that unraveled it all."

Casey's eyebrows raced to her forehead. "Oh, my god, the bloody footprint in the jury bathroom"

"Exactly right. I couldn't get the ATF's attention on that one, and I'd honestly let it go in my mind, until your problems with Judge Clarke over the damn disc. It didn't take much to figure out that whoever was putting pressure on the judge was working on McGinty's behalf, but not just his alone. Somebody had a big stake in keeping the sentencing mess quiet, and it was somebody who could get to the judge. And, I should add, it was somebody willing to kill. Not just once, but at least twice. We found Jack McGinty's body this morning slumped over the wheel of a car parked in the Rite Aid Drugstore lot. He'd been strangled."

Across the street an ambulance emerged from the garage ramp.

"And Ellis?" Casey turned her attention back to Luke.

"There was only one person I hadn't spoken to about all this, so after you threw me out of your house and your life, the stakes for me to solve this mess got very high. I went to see Judge Kanterman this morning. She's still not strong, but she let me challenge her memory of the night Ben died. She had buried most of it and had convinced herself that it had everything to do with the dog case. Then she remembered the tall guy behind the car. A tall, very tall man who looked vaguely familiar even in the dim light of the garage."

"Ellis. But why? What's the connection? It still doesn't make sense." Casey reached up instinctively to pull back her hair. It was a familiar and endearing gesture to Luke, and he felt an unwanted stirring. Looking down, he muttered to himself, "Bad time, bad place."

"That, Casey, is the jackpot question. We know now that Ellis, Ben, and McGinty were tied together by some enterprise, and we can assume, based on Ben's stash, that it involved Vicodin, and Oxy, and who knows what other painkillers and drugs. All three of those people are dead, and we're still clueless as to exactly why and who else is involved. And we have no idea what any of it has to do with the dog case or the bombing."

"My turn," said Casey with an impish look. When she had described in detail her encounter with the man waiting at the bottom of the stairwell, Luke nodded his head pensively. The perfect crew cut was showing more gray now than it had three weeks before, but Casey thought everyone aged a trace more under stress.

"So the British reporter is really just a bumbling ATF agent looking to smoke out the bomber?" Luke chuckled at his pun and then turned a serious face toward Casey. "Only one problem, Casey—the ATF pulled out of here when the case went to the jury, and I'm quite sure they left no one behind."

|62|

THERE ARE DAYS on Juno Beach that are so beautiful that they take your breath away. This was one of them, for sure. Ted Schuyler looked toward the water and decided he was a happy man. The Pizza Shop had done its usual business with the snowbirds and their pale-skinned grandkids from New Jersey. Now the white-hair-and-walkers crowd had headed home, and he could look forward to a few more months of relative calm.

He leaned down to lift the bag of leftover fertilizer. It was heavier that he'd expected, but then if he'd used any more of it, he'd have brought the whole damn courthouse down. And that was definitely not his plan. He simply wanted to teach some people a lesson. From what came over the news that night, he'd done a mighty good job of it, too.

"C'mon, Ted. If we don't leave soon, we'll miss the opening pitch." Ginny Schuyler poked her head around the door into the work shed. Her hair was cut boyishly short and made her look far younger than her years; that is, unless you picked up on the slivers of gray peeking through at her temples. "You can do that later. There's plenty of time."

Ted knew she was right. He had all the time in the world. The little roadside memorial to his baby girl was going to be there forever, and he'd plant it every year with the flowers that the local wildlife ignored for better sweets nearby.

They would take the long route to the baseball field where their son was playing with his traveling team. There was no need to talk about it. More than a year had passed since the accident, and it was still impossible for either of them to drive past the place. The fact that it happened so close to their home didn't surprise the police, but it added to their sense of powerlessness. "If only" seemed to begin every thought Ted had, and his most fervent hope had been that the drunken bastard who ran down his child would die himself in a jail cell.

His baby's death was one day he would not forget. And the day he was told that there would be no trial, there would be no plea in open court, and that the son of a bitch who ran her over like roadkill had been given probation was one he wouldn't forget either.

As he climbed behind the wheel of his pickup, Ted smiled with deep satisfaction. He knew he was a good man, a God-fearing man. He would never intentionally hurt a living soul. But somebody had to be accountable, and if the law couldn't or wouldn't do what was necessary . . . well, at least they should get shaken up a bit. It wasn't much, and it wouldn't bring his girl back, but it was better than nothing at all.

|EPILOGUE|

THE BRITISH REPORTER/ATF agent was never located. Local law enforcement, including Luke Anderson, gratefully turned the search for the man's whereabouts and identity over to the Feds.

Following the wounding of Judge Clarke and the murder of her husband, the "Dogicide" case was finally declared a mistrial. A new trial has not been scheduled. Lloyd Schwartzman has appealed the case, claiming that a new trial would violate the U.S. Consitution as it would place his client in double jeopardy. Josiah Diemert remains free on bond. The whereabouts of Butch, Josiah's pit bull dog, are unknown.

Janet Kanterman returned to the bench and, with the concurrence of the presiding judge, determined that Judge

Clarke could not fire Casey, as Casey was hired by Kanterman, and only Kanterman could dismiss her.

Luke and Casey have no immediate plans to live together. Casey has applied to the Palm Beach County Sheriff's Office and will take the entrance exam in the Spring.

Barbara Clarke resigned from the bench and faces disciplinary action for her failure to report threats against her and, by extension, to the court as a whole.

Harold Cohen is serving a two- to five-year sentence for voluntary manslaughter in the Florida State Penitentiary.

Miriam Cohen has moved to Arizona to be closer to her granddaughter, Amy.

The courthouse bomber has never been found.

BLAME

|PROLOGUE|

IT IS NOT true, as some observers of the human drama postulate, that blame is the handmaiden of punishment. The two are barely on speaking terms, especially in a court of law. Recognizing the on-again, off-again connection between fixing responsibility for bad behavior and devising a suitable punishment for it has bedeviled scholars of criminal law for centuries. It has also perplexed more than a handful of theologians and philosophers. It is not surprising, therefore, that the death of a young man, ostensibly in his prime, and for no apparent reason, has aroused the passions of residents of the Treasure Coast as they cast about, searching for the source of this villainy. Someone must take the blame.

Enter the prosecution. Charlie Graham has successfully

prosecuted a baker's dozen of major trials in his seven years as State Attorney. The "Dog Case" is the outstanding exception, although it is still on appeal to the Florida Supreme Court. Despite what Charlie views as an almost perfect record of putting away the bad guys, he faces a serious challenge for reelection next year. Charlie needs a case with sex appeal, muscle, and a touch of mother's milk. What better than the untimely demise of a victim of the notorious pain pill industry in West Palm Beach? The fact that the victim came from a well-heeled Jewish family living in a gated community added immeasurably to the appeal of the case—and its potential for sizeable campaign contributions.

Charlie's wife, who attends all of his closing arguments at trial, has complained to her mother on more than one occasion that Charlie is so self-absorbed that he misses the big picture, to say nothing of her birthdays and their anniversaries. Her observation is astute, because Charlie will once again fail to anticipate the full measure of mischief that bringing an indictment for first-degree murder in this case will bring about.

1

THE BUZZ WAS wearing off. He was beginning that downward spiral again, the dip into the black hole that his psychiatrist liked to call "Dante's Inferno." His depression felt more like an insatiable animal, feeding on his thoughts until only the brittle bones of his despair and self-hatred remained behind. Even if the insistent pain he suffered from his back injuries disappeared overnight, he knew that the internal injuries to his self-esteem were incurable. During his adolescence, a handful of shrinks had tried to convince him that his problems were treatable with the right medications. When he dropped out of college, the counselor had almost begged him to sign up for just one course so she could continue his therapy sessions. Everyone tried to help. No one had succeeded or ever would succeed. Not now, not ever.

He reached over to the glass table that served as his nightstand and grabbed two of the dozen or so pill bottles that sat on top. What he took, or how much he took, no longer mattered to him. "Just get me the fuck out," he whimpered, not wanting to alarm his parents, presumably asleep in the next room. "I hope everybody blames her. The bitch deserves it."

It suddenly struck him that without a suicide note, they might not understand why he'd done this—that her betrayal was the last one he could or would bear. Stupid. How could he be so stupid as to come back home tonite and off himself without a fucking note? The cunt dumped him at the altar and nobody would know he died because of it—because of her.

His chest began to heave as the panic set in. He raised himself up in the twin bed, but suddenly he realized that his body had not moved. Now he was scared, really scared. It was time to cave, to call his parents and play out this ridiculous "from the precipice" scene again. Too bad he didn't have the guts to go through with it. He called out. But, no sound came. He inhaled deeply. But, nothing happened. His eyes rolled up to look at the Spiderman figure that had hung from the ceiling fan since his childhood. And then he died.

By the time Casey got the call, the body had passed through rigor mortis. Jeffrey Klausner was not found until the morning after his suicide, and according to his distraught parents, it was not his failure to appear for breakfast but the terrible stench emanating from his room that aroused their concern. Casey was a rookie, and it showed on her face when she walked into the room. She'd never had a brother, but she had strong connections with her sister and parents, and she cringed inwardly at the thought of finding a sibling or child dead by his own hand. She looked over her shoulder at her partner, Simon Rivera, saw his bland and professional demeanor, and vowed to work harder to achieve this mature appearance in even the most difficult circumstances.

They sat in the kitchen with the parents while the forensics teams did their work upstairs. Casey was amazed at the amount of time and detail involved in doing a proper job at a crime scene. Her work prior to attending the police academy was as bailiff to a circuit court judge at the West Palm Beach Justice Complex. She remembered her impatience with policemen who griped about the time they were required to waste sitting in the hallway outside the courtroom, waiting for what was often only a few minutes of testimony. Even worse was the long wait for a case in which the defendant decided at the last minute to plead and avoid a trial. She now understood their frustration, especially since it was often a rookie who was assigned to a preliminary hearing or a simple drug case.

Once the detectives arrived, she and Simon could go back to the station and write the incident report, a seemingly benign name to describe something that ended in someone's death. She looked over at Mrs. Klausner and immediately regretted it. The woman returned her gaze and said in response to no one, "I knew it. I knew it, and I begged him to end it. That girl was poison. She killed my son."

Her husband reached over and squeezed her shoulder. "Be quiet, Myrna. Don't talk like that. That's crazy talk. People break up all the time, and they don't kill themselves over it."

The porcelain dish flew off the table and crashed against the early American wood cabinets before falling in pieces to the floor. "You can goddamn call it what you want, Harold. I don't care if he tried before. He always knew to stop. He always called for us. She killed him, as if she'd pulled out a knife and stabbed him in the heart." Myrna Klausner put her hand over her heart and gasped. "She's killing me too."

Myrna wasn't clairvoyant, but this time her premonitions were pretty good.

|2|

WHILE MYRNA KLAUSNER was arguing with Casey Portman and the other police officers on the scene about taking her son's body to the Myerhoff Funeral Home instead of the Coroner's Office, the news of the tragedy began to spread, but not quickly enough to reach everyone who had a reason to know. It didn't get to Lovey in time, and she had plenty of reason to know.

Lovey Nussbaum had a short list of people and things she admired. Thin definitely topped the list. Anyone who knew her well could attest to her devotion to all things emaciated. So obsessed was she with this particular virtue that it was impossible to be in her company for more than a few

233

minutes without a dissertation on the latest diet and exercise regimen.

Her two children, Scott and Marcy, made the list, but her older sister did not. Her parents, Eli and Margaret Jessup, had died so long ago that they rarely crossed her mind other than to remind her of how very far she had come from the aluminum-sided, one-bathroom, linoleum-floored shack that they had called home. Including them was out of the question.

Leonard Nussbaum, the engineer of her meteoric rise in socioeconomic status, made the list, but barely. His success-ful practice as a urologist was certainly a factor in his favor, but his lackluster performance in bed, a skill that to this day Lovey firmly believed should have improved with maturity and tutoring, was a black mark against his standing in her estimation. Hence, an ambivalent and grudging last place on the short list.

The remaining three slots were reserved for her best friends, Sissy, Joan, and Nina, and for the attributes they shared, namely their sense of loyalty, good hair, and clear skin.

It was in pursuit of this last value—clear skin—that Lovey had booked an early morning appointment with her cosmetician. The morning sun, struggling to pulse through the fog, would find her frantically racing from room to room, from window to window, like a flipbook of pictures, looking for her car keys. As she rounded the corner to the laundry room, her right foot (the one Lenny insisted was malformed near the ankle) skated onto the woven rug from Tibet, riding with her as she was momentarily airborne before slamming into the washer and dryer.

It would be malicious to suggest that a day would come when people would wish for Lovey just such a Tibetan rug-sailing mishap. But all these things were in the future. As was the murder. For the present, Lovey was yelling for help, rubbing her sore, rapidly swelling kneecap, and wondering how in God's name she was supposed to show up for a rehearsal dinner for her daughter, an admittedly testy young woman who was engaged to a sophomoric boy named Jeff Klausner, with two zits on her cheekbone and a broken knee.

In hindsight, she should have seen these misfortunes as omens. Hadn't the foul-smelling, greasy-haired rug salesman in Tibet assured Lenny that the rug had mystical powers? Lenny shouldn't have snorted at that. Not only was it impolite to make light of these peoples' religious beliefs, but if it was true, his cynical blunder may also have brought a curse into their home.

Something must have.

|3|

THE EXECUTIVE CHEF at La Mer Country Club had fled the town of Lucca in western Italy approximately five minutes before the girl's father and the local *polizia* arrived at his door. His mother had saved his life once again, but he knew this was the last time. Thank God his brother was the assistant pastry chef at a swank gated community in Palm Beach Gardens, Florida. Marco's papers for a work permit had been approved in the nick of time—unlike his withdrawal from the delicious interior of the waitress at La Prima Trattoria set into the outer walls of the Old City.

He was a handsome man, but he was short in stature. In Italy this was by no means a fatal flaw for romantic adventures. But the largely Jewish population at La Mer seemed to view it as an anomaly. They were from the East Coast, which he soon learned meant New York or New Jersey. And they had very clear and well-articulated expectations. Among these were the belief that all Italians were good cooks, good lovers, and tall.

Just now, the man from Lucca, Marco Guarino, was mostly a pissed-off Italian. His back was to the wall of a large and impressively decorated dining room. In keeping with the name of the community, the motif was mockingly French, with *étoile* prints, carved arms on plump velveteen chairs, and tapestries hanging everywhere possible. All of it was faux, of course, but the residents loved it. And Marco loved the residents. He had risen in no time at all from sous chef to dining room chef to Executive Chef. His salary was spectacular, considering his qualifications and experience, and both he and his brother, now the head of catering, were regarded as indispensable.

But today, he had a major problem. He had just received word that the event planned for tonight, a rehearsal dinner for three hundred guests, would have to be canceled. "Not possible!" he shouted into the phone, looking around the kitchen area for something to throw. Storming into the ornate dining room, he surveyed the perfectly laid tables, complete with stemware for champagne and five flights of fine wines. "Spare no expense," his brother had said, and Marco had not. The caviar was chilling in the gigantic refrigerators downstairs, alongside the stone crab claws, the tenderloins, and the *haricots vert*. On a prep table nearby lay the pungent greens, the small candles, the charger plates and, of course, the fancy sparklers for the Baked Alaska. Most of this elaborate meal would end up in the employees' lunchroom, a bonanza for them but a goddamn disaster for him. The Nussbaums were hosting this rehearsal dinner, and they were among the most difficult members of the club. He had no illusions about whether Leonard and Lovey would ante up the whole cost for a celebration gone sour. "*Not a chance,*" he thought, smacking the marble serving table with the flat of his hand.

But Marco was nothing if not resourceful. These people loved to eat, he mused, whatever the occasion. The wine could be saved for another time, but what could be more healing after this tragedy than a shared meal after the funeral for the groom?

Nurturing, perhaps. But "healing?" Not if you include the fist fight over the smoked salmon.

TO BE CONTINUED

CPSIA information can be obtained at www.ICGtesting.com
Printed in the USA
LVOW061420220313

325520LV00001B/66/P